SQUARE
FISH

An Imprint of Macmillan

VOTE FOR LARRY. Copyright © 2004 by Janet Tashjian. All rights reserved.
Printed in the United States of America. For information, address
Square Fish, 175 Fifth Avenue, New York, N.Y. 10010.

Square Fish and the Square Fish logo are trademarks of Macmillan
and are used by Henry Holt and Company under license from Macmillan.

Library of Congress Cataloging-in-Publication Data
Tashjian, Janet.
Vote for Larry / Janet Tashjian.
p.   cm.
Sequel to: The gospel according to Larry.
Summary: Not yet eighteen years old, Josh, a.k.a. Larry, comes out of hiding
and returns to public life, this time to run for president as an advocate
for issues of concern to youth and to encourage voter turnout.
[1. Elections—Fiction.   2. Politics, Practical—Fiction.
3. Political activists—Fiction.]   I. Title.
PZ7.T211135Vo2004   [Fic]—dc22   2003056578

ISBN-13: 978-0-312-38446-3
ISBN-10: 0-312-38446-7

Originally published in the United States by Henry Holt and Company, LLC
Square Fish logo designed by Filomena Tuosto
First Square Fish Edition: September 2008
10 9 8 7 6 5 4 3 2 1
www.squarefishbooks.com

VOTE FOR LARRY

Janet Tashjian

SQUARE
FISH

HENRY HOLT

For Janine

Prologue

"No way," I told the young man standing in my driveway.

"Come on," he said. "You *have* to."

"I already wrote that book."

"Technically, you didn't write it. I wrote it." He smiled. "But I've got another story to tell."

"You're the best person to tell your story. I told you that last time."

"But you did such a good job getting the word out with *The Gospel According to Larry*."

"Sure, but when the book was published I couldn't find you. People couldn't tell if it was a true story or if I made it up. . . ."

"Are you asking me to feel bad for you? You got the best reviews of your career!"

I pulled Josh aside. "I looked everywhere. You obviously didn't want to be found."

"I've been through a lot since I saw you," he answered.

"I know you have—do you think I live under a rock?"

"You're mad at me," he said.

"I'm not mad. I'm just…" As I looked at Josh's unshaven face, shoulder-length hair, and Sea-Monkeys T-shirt, it was hard to stay mad for long. "You did a lot of good—again."

"Yeah, after some serious false starts."

"We all have those."

He reached into his pack and handed me a CD.

"Is this music?" I asked.

He shook his head. "Data."

"Oh no," I said. "Is there a sign hanging around my neck that says SECRETARY?"

"You owe me."

I tried to find a technicality. "I write young-adult books. It's more than two years since *Larry*; what are you now, almost twenty?"

"Pretend I'm a fictional character. You can make me seventeen again, easy."

"Well, I live in the *non*fiction world," I said.

"Make it up! Isn't that what writers do?"

I told him it was a little more complicated than that.

I stared at the disc in my hand and wondered what I'd be getting myself into.

"I realize the world changes every second," he said. "But everything in here is accurate as of today."

"We'll fact-check anyway. But there aren't footnotes, are there? The typesetters went nuts last time."

His huge grin reminded me of my son's. "So you'll do it, right?"

Visions of my own work came and left. I nodded and told him I would.

"You can't call me," he said. "I'll call you."

I looked at this boy—part stranger, part intimate friend. "So what's new?" I asked.

His eyes sparkled and he grinned. "Everything."

VOTE FOR
LARRY

PART ONE

"Our lives begin to end the day we become
silent about things that matter."

Dr. Martin Luther King Jr.

Boulder was beautiful.

Nestled in the Rockies, with clear, comfortable weather and lots of college students, it was the perfect place for me to settle into a semi-normal, anonymous life.

I rented a room in a Victorian-type bungalow north of the University of Colorado campus, where the hundred-year-old architecture and tree-lined streets reminded me of my home back in Massachusetts. My three housemates were nice, all students at C.U. If the media circus two years ago hadn't forced me to disappear, I'd be at Princeton now, boning up on Kant and Nietzsche. But most days, I didn't mind how my life and future had been waylaid because I never would've ended up in such a wondrous place.

Even though I'd been here for several months, the Flatirons still took me by surprise. Back home I'd been to New Hampshire and Maine to hike in the mountains many times, but living smack-dab in the middle of them was a whole different experience.

I wasn't the only person who felt this way; pretty much everyone who lived out here engaged in daily outdoor activity, as if not partaking in the immense beauty would be a sinful waste. Even the biggest computer nerd[1] hiked, biked, or canoed daily. Living in Boulder was like one prolonged recess.

Because enough time had gone by and the Larry furor had dissipated,[2] I let my hair return to its original brown. When people asked where I was from, I said my father was a consultant and we'd traveled around a lot. I explained that my family was now in Chicago and I didn't visit much. The name I used was Mark Paulson.

After dissecting the fall catalog on the floor of my room, I decided to concentrate my efforts not in philosophy as I'd always planned, but in the field of environmental, population, and organismic biology.[3] The country's flora and fauna had nurtured me for most of my life; it seemed like an area of study that made sense. And it only took a few days at the EPOB department to realize I wanted to focus on animal behavior. I'd read several books on ethology for fun and had to suppress my enthusiasm in class each time the professor posed a question.[4] I carried around my textbook like some zoological Rosetta stone, making notes in the margins daily.

I'd been painfully vigilant about never using my real name and paying for everything in cash from my various jobs, but the thought of enrolling in an institution still scared the life out of

---

[1]That would be me. . . .

[2]Unexpected worship for my anti-consumer Web site resulting in me faking my own death. The usual senior-year routine.

[3]Conservation, biodiversity, environmental protection, to name a few.

[4]Story of my life.

me. Instead I sat in on classes and volunteered in the research lab without credit.

I had other projects, of course: the Inspirational Quote Word Search I'd created in fractals class and the Greek mythology flip-o-rama comic.[5]

I was living in nature and learning lots of new things. Life was good.

And when I met Janine, it shot straight to ecstatic.

I was trading three old CDs for new ones at my favorite used-record store on the Hill.[6] I spotted her at the register— black sneakers, torn jeans, and earrings made from two fuzzy dice like the kind some people hung from their rear-view mirror.

"How's it going?" I asked.

She smiled but didn't answer.

"I loved this Beck," I said. "Hate to give it up."

She nodded, still no words. I figured she was shy.

"Did the new Santana come in?"

She pointed to the rack of new releases.

"Do you . . . ?" I trailed off, not sure what I wanted to say.

She reached behind the register and held up an index card. PLEASE RESPECT MY SILENCE. IT'S MY PERSONAL STATEMENT TO COMBAT THE BARRAGE OF WORDS THAT ASSAULT US EACH DAY.

I held my finger to my lips. A woman after my own heart.

---

[5]A guy needs hobbies, right?

[6]Yes, I still owned fewer than seventy-five possessions, in constant rotation.

7

"Do you do this all the time?" I asked. "You can just nod if you want to."

She turned the card over and wrote EVERY MONDAY.

I thanked her for the three-CD credit and left the store. Tomorrow was Tuesday, a much better day to pick out new CDs.

The next afternoon when we went for coffee, Janine wouldn't shut up. She talked nonstop about her poli sci classes, her family back in Seattle, the Hives concert she'd been to over the weekend. Turns out we both volunteered at the local PIRG office, canvassing and making phone calls for various consumer and environmental causes. She talked about how she'd been silent on Mondays for more than five years—a day to reflect without the distraction of speech. But after an hour and a half together, I came to the conclusion that the barrage of words Janine needed a weekly respite from was her own.

Still, she was adorable—great sense of humor, a slight stutter when she got excited, the most bizarre taste in clothes I'd ever seen. (She wore a yellow vinyl BMX jacket with splattered painter's pants and cocktail swizzle sticks tucked into her streaked hair.)

Since I'd left Boston, I had barely gone out with anyone, but Janine seemed worth the risk. I asked her if she wanted to come over Friday night to watch a movie.

She did, then left three days later.

• • •

The next several weeks were filled with late-night conversations, hikes up Mount Sanitas, and silent Mondays. I walked her collie, Brady, on the nights she had to work. The last time I was this happy, I was sitting in my basement swing back home, composing Larry's sermons. Now I was high on the mountains of Colorado and my first real girlfriend.[7]

"Come on! Come on!" Janine grabbed my arm and pulled me toward the Fox Theatre. The Samples were back in town and she didn't want to miss one note.

Music was like oxygen to Janine; she couldn't go more than a few minutes without it. She knew people at every concert site within a hundred-mile radius; she got tickets way before those babies hit Ticketmaster. And always the best seats. When she jumped up and down during a show, the look on her face bordered on someone witnessing a miracle. Lucky for me, her joy was contagious.

The simplicity of what made her smile was a welcome change from how much I'd always expected from the world. She loved to sit with Brady and watch *The Planet's Funniest Animals*. Me? Not content till the world was at peace, till every worker earned enough to make a decent living. It was almost a relief to settle in after a day of classes to watch someone's cockatoo walk across piano keys, trying to sing.

But even with our differences, we got along fine. I came this close to telling her about the whole Larry business but decided that was a piece of baggage no relationship could withstand.

---

[7]Don't bring up Beth; it's still a sore subject.

Anyone who knew me growing up would look at her and marvel at the resemblance to someone important in my life— my no-longer-with-us mother.

Not just the dark hair and the big, loud laugh, but her open and slightly manic view of the world. Sometimes the similarities were scary. When Janine brought home CDs from the store, she might as well have lifted them from my mother's album collection. Between the music and her retro clothes, the surge of memories almost knocked me across the room.

I felt like I'd come home. Except for one small thing.

Her favorite thing to do on Saturdays?

Shop.

These were the times I almost told her about Larry. Almost told her I'd had a Web site devoted to anti-consumerism, that thousands—then millions—of kids from around the world had joined me in my quest to be non-materialistic. That I'd kept my number of possessions down to seventy-five for almost four years now—didn't she notice I wore the same clothes all the time? That I'd dropped out of society because *I* began to be consumed. That asking me to go shopping was like gnawing on a leg of lamb in front of a group of card-carrying vegetarians. *That I just couldn't do it!*

At first I tried to reason with her: How could someone who volunteered ten hours a week for an activist organization spend her free time loading up on things she didn't need? She'd say she earned her money and could decide how to spend it. She even felt that buying dresses at a vintage store was a form of recycling. I told her spending was spending; we even broke up twice because of our differing philosophies. But each time I left her apartment, the piece of me that still ached for some semblance of home begged me to call Janine back to patch things up. We always did.

So we reached a type of compromise: On those Saturdays I didn't have to work in the bakery, she could drag me to her favorite stores.[8] But I would not—under any circumstances—buy anything.

It was more difficult than I thought.

Here's the part I'm almost too embarrassed to write about, that I'm revealing only in my quest to (a) understand myself better and (b) be honest with you.

I began to like going shopping.

Usually when I walked through the Pearl Street Mall,[9] it was to enjoy the fresh air and the abundant opportunities to people watch. But once I actually went *into* stores, I realized how out-of-the-loop I was in pretty much every department of pop culture. So while Janine was trying on lipstick,[10] I killed time by browsing until browsing became interesting in and of itself.

Some of the stuff was fun—T-shirts with witty sayings, aerodynamically designed kites, fountains that emanated tranquility.

---

[8] I loved my old job at the bookstore but given my situation I thought it might be too risky working with a bookish crowd.

[9] It's not a MALL mall, but a long semi-touristy promenade where everyone in town hangs out.

[10] I told you she reminded me of my mom.

The whole shopping experience was less painful than I thought it would be.

I was looking but not buying, an important distinction.

Yet it wasn't the browsing that led to my downfall.

It was Janine's thoughtful one-month anniversary present.

She walked into my bedroom carrying a large striped gift bag. Inside the bag were eleven CDs, straight from the late-night conversations we'd had about my mother's musical taste. Jimi Hendrix, Joni Mitchell, Marvin Gaye, U2[11]—all of whom contributed to my musical education. I thanked her profusely, then we stayed up all night listening to them. I was in aural nostalgic heaven, but one thought kept returning: *You can't keep these and stay at seventy-five possessions. You have to get rid of them.*

But I couldn't.[12] I spent the next morning making a list of which of my old items to jettison. To keep the CDs, I'd be down to one pair of pants, three pairs of socks, two shirts, almost no books. . . .

And here is where I admit my crime, along with my deep sense of shame.

I kept the CDs.

And the rest of my possessions.

And that, fellow pilgrim, was the beginning of the end.

---

[11]Janine would've gone nuts if she knew the part Bono had played in my past life.
[12]HOW DO YOU SAY NO TO ALL THAT GREAT MUSIC?!

Ahhh, the physics of the downward spiral.

I mean, if you're at eighty-six possessions, what's a few more to get you to an even hundred? I'd been at seventy-five possessions for years, and where had it gotten me besides semi-deprived and out of touch with my peers?[13]

Advertising and consumerism creep up on you slowly, lulling you into thinking nothing is happening until it's too late. Like staying at the beach all day without sunscreen; you don't realize you're burned till you've enjoyed what you thought was a fabulous day. Then, of course, you're screwed.

It wasn't long before I looked forward to accompanying Janine on her little outings to a vintage store or REI. And then, following the laws of physics, it was only a matter of time before gravity forced me to make my first purchases.[14] The creativity I brought to justifying my new items was limitless. I _needed_ that Gore-Tex windbreaker—didn't it get chilly hiking in the mountains in the early evening? And if I had a few extra

---

[13]Don't be too horrified; it gets worse.
[14]I told you it got worse.

pairs of pants, I wouldn't have to go to the Laundromat so often and could get more work done, right? The excuses and rationalizations for what I knew was excessive spending astounded me. It happened slowly, but it happened nonetheless. The final proof that I had completely abandoned all my principles was when I received my pre-approved credit card in the mail.[15]

Janine liked to talk about *spaving* money, a philosophy based on the theory that the more money you *spent* on sale items, the more money you *saved*. She'd march into my room with several shopping bags, bragging about how much money she'd spaved that afternoon. I'd re-wrap the items in their tissue and ask her how much she'd *spent*.

From the outside, I looked content and well-dressed.

Inside, I was dying—too depressed to even do my morning yoga.

Here's what I thought about while I lay awake most nights: How can you take part in this vibrant culture of ours *and* honor your principles? How do you balance the stimulation of the outside world with the tranquility of your interior landscape? Is that what life is—a constant tug-of-war between the external and the internal? And more important, have I become one of the people I despise?[16]

---

[15] I couldn't believe how easy it was to get one; even Brady got offers from every bank in town. You don't want to hear about how I held the card up to the light, watching the holographic square change colors, rubbing my fingers across the raised letters of the name that was just as fake as I was.

[16] Don't answer that.

I guess the thing I thought about most was the formula for life's happiness. It seemed to me there was a direct correlation between how happy (or unhappy) you were and how authentically you were living. I wasn't being authentic to my beliefs, and it showed. But did that make me change my behavior, mend my so-called ways?

No.

I'm ashamed to say that I was so relieved to finally have a girlfriend that I continued to stuff my real feelings and beliefs into a metaphorical laundry bag stashed in the back of my closet.

Janine was worried.

"Mark, what's wrong with you?"

Even though I'd been using the alias for months, I still had to remind myself to answer to the name Mark. I told her everything was fine.

"You're not fine. You're miserable." She climbed into my lap and played with my hair. "This isn't like you."

I'll tell you what isn't me, I thought. It isn't like me to be wearing an Abercrombie & Fitch T-shirt with jeans that say Diesel across my ass. It isn't like me to waste valuable Saturday afternoons inside stores that underpay their workers, to say nothing of the Asian slave laborers who made all this stuff. Of course it *was* like me to *think* it and not *say* it. That passive-aggressive, don't-say-what-you-mean nonsense was buried in the DNA of the real me: Josh Swensen. And when I spotted Janine's copy of Thoreau's *Walden* on the table, I dove across the room to turn it over. My hero's face staring out at me from the cover was too much to bear.

With every new purchase, I became more and more miserable. Instead of being honest with Janine, I did something cowardly, unthinkable.

I began to compare her to Beth.

Beth had haunted my psyche since sixth grade, why should she stop now just because we were two thousand miles apart?[17] You would think that having a great girlfriend like Janine would dilute some of those Beth feelings, make her fade farther and farther into the background of my mind. But strangely enough, going out with Janine actually made my Beth-fascination worse. *Beth would never make videotapes of her dog to send to a lame TV show. Beth would never yak on a cell phone while flipping through a rack of shirts at Urban Outfitters.* These comparisons weren't fair to Janine, but they ran through my mind like some lovesick ticker tape. And when December 5 rolled around, I had no choice but to succumb.

Beth and I used to gag at the fake holidays the greeting card companies invented to get people to buy cards. Our favorite—even more than "International Hug Day"—was "Play Hooky from Work to Go Holiday Shopping Day." Every December 5 for years, we goofed on such a ridiculous, manufactured event. Last year, a few months after my pseudocide, I couldn't help but call her from a pay phone on the road in Nashville. I realized she might be at Brown, but given it was a Saturday, I took a chance.[18]

---

[17]And let's not forget the fact that she thought I was dead—a minor inconvenience to any successful relationship.

[18]Punching those familiar numbers into the keypad was the most rewarding moment I'd had on the road up until that point, believe me.

Beth's hello made me hang up the phone quicker than if it had been on fire. I jumped on the next bus out of town, scared but empowered by the sound of her voice.

This year, I used another pay phone and a pre-paid calling card that couldn't be traced.

I slipped off my Nike jacket before I dialed, as if Beth's spirit could see me through the telephone wires. I ignored the part of me that felt like I was cheating on Janine.

"Hello?"

Beth's voice shot through me like a wayward rocket; I hung up quickly, willing the words "Happy Hooky Day" to the familiar red wall phone hanging in Beth's kitchen back in Boston.

Hearing Beth again brought back a flood of memories. The tabloid stories and crush of reporters outside my door after betagold outed me.[19] These thoughts always led to a low-grade panic that bloomed into a full-fledged paranoia I'd grown to recognize. I'd check out other kids in class, wondering if any of them were working for betagold or the *National Enquirer*. And what about Janine—could the shopping trips be a trap? During these bouts of fear, I'd start talking to myself or fall asleep at the bakery's kneading table.

I told myself things couldn't get any worse.

Then I got my first credit card bill.

---

[19]Betagold: a sixty-year-old woman named Tracy Hawthorne who became obsessed with exposing Larry's true identity. Get a life!

$847.24?!

Are you kidding me?

I did the math: If you charged $2,000 on one credit card and faithfully made the minimum payment every month, it would take you eleven years to pay it off. *Eleven years!* You would have paid more than $4,000 on those original purchases, even if you never used the card again. The only thing that made sense was for me to take this invoice and pay off the $847.24 in full.

But I didn't have the money.

Between making minimum wage, taxes, and the cost of living, I could barely scrape together the monthly payment. I had to take on a second job in a video store just to pay off all this STUFF.

I complained to Janine on our way back from the movies.

"You get used to the bills," she said. "It's like this for everybody."

"No, it's not. I know plenty of people our age who aren't slaves to debt." Of course, the person I was thinking of was Beth.

Janine shrugged. "Life is short—you should enjoy it."

"Yeah, paying off credit cards—that's my idea of fun."

"You're such a spoilsport. It's the holidays, Mark, come on!"

. . .

But the credit card and the debt only increased my anxiety. From the back room of the bakery, I checked out who was in line at the counter up front. I began to delete any sites I visited on the Web, using the latest software to cover my e-tracks. I wondered if betagold had ever gotten down off the Larry Conspiracy soapbox.[20]

I even stole an old trick from the movies and stuck a match between the door and the jamb in case anyone tried to break into my room while I was out. It became habit to check it each morning and afternoon.

"You're insane," Janine said. "Completely adorable."

I didn't want to be adorable; I wanted to be safe.

Six days later, after coming back from hiking, I stared at my door in disbelief. The match was on the floor, bent in half.

I backed away from the door and hurried over to Janine's.

One thing about Janine—she never could keep a straight face.

"Mark, relax! It was me! You were being so ridiculous, I *had* to."

---

[20]It was hard for me to truly despise her I-don't-believe-Larry-is-dead speeches. After all, she was *right*.

A few months ago, I would have thought this was funny. But I was not amused.

"You've been acting crazy lately," she said. "Worried about having a credit card, about someone breaking into your room. What's next—a secret identity?"

I headed back to Mount Sanitas and broke my own record on the ascent.

As I sat on the ledge overlooking Boulder, I wondered how I could have become so distant from my own life, barely the Josh/Larry/Mark who had moved here months ago. I did a mental Ben Franklin list: on the plus side, I had a girlfriend. I liked having someone imaginative and smart in my life; it had been something I'd daydreamed about all those years I'd been staring at my computer screen back home. And my new field of study was challenging and rewarding.

On the minus side, I was living a life diametrically opposed to my belief system—or was I? Maybe all those theories I'd been spouting on my old Web site weren't the real me at all. Maybe I was a consumer zombie all along, pretending I wasn't. No matter which way I analyzed it, I felt like a giant fake.

The sweater I was wearing, a present from Janine on one of her preppy days, had POLO emblazoned across the chest in giant blue letters. I felt like a cow—branded, letters burned into my skin—telling the world who my owner was. I tore the sweater off, left it on the rock, and headed back down the mountain.

On my descent, I almost bumped into a guy my age on his way up. He was wrapped in several layers to ward off the evening winds. He eyed me in my T-shirt.

"Dude, aren't you cold?"

I shook my head, in no mood to talk. By the time I got back to my bike, I was shivering, but not from the weather.

I hoped I had the courage to change my own life—again.

I had given up the match trick after Janine's little prank, but I hadn't given up the vigilance. That night, I peeked through the blinds and checked up and down the street for any strange cars. I made sure I was the last one to sleep in the house and locked the front door.

It didn't do any good.

I woke up the second the door to my room clicked open. I jumped out of bed but was quickly knocked over by someone in the room. He[21] pushed me back down on the bed and quickly tied my hands behind my back. When I screamed for my housemates, he pulled out a roll of duct tape, snapped off a length, and covered my mouth. I shouted NO! as the tape closed around me. Another masked intruder looked through my closet and drawers, throwing my stuff into a box—laptop, books, backpack, a few clothes.

Okay, I thought. It's just a robbery; there are burglaries around campus all the time. It's not because you're Larry; it's *not*. Let them take what they want and leave. I tried to let the dangerous thoughts—*betagold, betagold*—simmer down in another part of my mind.

The intruder lifted me to my feet—my attempt at making

---

[21]I say "he" because the person was about my size, but his face was covered by a hooded mask.

myself dead weight was obviously not working—and shoved me toward the door. Visions of tabloid headlines filled my head in twenty-point font: HOAX! GURU LARRY ALIVE. I fought him every step of the way.

The two people worked quickly and efficiently, one carrying my shoulders, the other my legs. Outside in the darkness, they shoved me into the backseat of a car parked across the street. One jumped behind the wheel; the other climbed in next to me. When the big one pulled off his mask to drive, I studied his face: beard, my age, focused. I hoped his face wasn't the last thing I'd see on this earth.

Then the kidnapper sitting next to me reached for his hood. Of all the faces that had flashed before me in the three minutes since they had burst into my room, this one was not on the list.

It was Beth.

"Nautica pajamas. Really, Josh." She barked out driving directions to the guy behind the wheel. "Take a right, Simon—70 East."

I tried to talk through the tape, a jumble of grunts and noise.

"Forget it," Beth said. "It's your turn to listen."

I wondered if she could tell I was grinning underneath the tape. Beth! God, I *missed* her.

"I apologize for the drama—it was Simon's idea. He didn't think you'd come willingly. Plus, he thought it might be fun."

"A bit of the old fraternity hazing, hey, old friend?" His accent was high-end British, maybe Cambridge or Oxford. I wanted to rip the tape off but couldn't.

Beth looked at me kindly, then belted me in the arm. Hard.

"You let me think you were *dead*! I cried every night for months!"

Now *this* was worth listening to.

"You were selfish and cruel and I hate you. What do you have to say for yourself?"

I arched my eyebrows in an attempt to illustrate the obvious. She ripped off the duct tape in the same way my mother used to rip off a Band-Aid: no coaxing, just fast, sharp pain.

"Beth," I said after the sting wore off. "I'm so sorry."

"You should be." She reminded me of her stubborn and gorgeous grade-school self.

"When did you figure it out?" I asked.

"I was home for the weekend last year, totally thinking of you on Blow Off Work and Shop Day when the phone rang. No one was there, and I just *knew.*"

"I didn't stay on the phone long enough for a trace. Besides that was last year, and I was in Tennessee!"

"Then *The Gospel According to Larry* came out and I was sure of it. So I put together a plan and waited."

"A year?!"

She looked pretty pleased with herself. "I took this semester off for independent study, then hired a security company to put a trap line on my parents' phone December 5. It records every call that comes in—blocked calls, pay phones, cells. It cost me a hundred dollars an hour, but I knew you'd call again. I got a printout the next day with all the numbers that had come in, and there was one from Colorado no one recognized. I flew out to Denver, hired an investigator, gave her your photo—it didn't take long after that. Simon's at Harvard this year, so he drove out to meet me."

Of course Beth would be the one to find me. It only made sense that she'd put our platonic telepathy to good use. My love for Beth had been my Achilles heel my whole life. Why should things be any different while I was underground? And here she was in the flesh.

"I never thought I'd see you again." Then I made the mistake of reaching over to kiss her.

Simon swerved into the breakdown lane so quickly, three cars behind us almost collided. He lunged into the backseat. "What the hell is going on?" he asked.

"Simon, you're acting like a caveman," Beth said. "Knock it off."

I looked at Beth, not caring what Simon was feeling. "You two?"

"We've been together almost a year," she said. "Simon was one of the keynotes at the Global Debt Conference." She reached for his arm reassuringly. "Duckie, there's nothing to worry about."[22]

He put his blinker on to re-enter the lane. "You okay, little rabbit?"

"Are you talking to me?" I asked.

Beth elbowed me again.

"If you two don't knock off the baby talk, I'll jump out of the car, I swear."

Simon ignored me and began driving again.

Well, I guess some things never change. Beth told Simon I was "nothing to worry about." That pretty much summed up my relationship with her in a nutshell. And Simon—good looking, at Harvard, and with an impossible-to-compete-with British accent.

---

[22]Duckie? Was she serious?

Duckie? Please let this be a nightmare and I wake up back in Boulder. But when I looked at Beth again, I knew I'd rather be in an absurd nightmare with her than in any kind of reality without her.

She pulled a three-ring binder from her bag. "Simon and I have done a lot of amazing things together." She tallied up their accomplishments—candidates getting elected, workers' rights, legislation passed. I could feel myself shrink into the seat; while Janine and I had been circling the outlet stores for parking spaces, Beth and Simon had actually made a difference in the world. I saw myself through her eyes and thought about how silly and superficial I must seem. Larry had been the impetus to open the doors of activism for her,[23] and now she had left me in the dust. And as much as I felt like I'd let the world down by not contributing, a small piece of my mind fixated on something else. Something personal.

Beth had a boyfriend.

And it still wasn't me.

---

[23]Okay, you got me. She had these beliefs before Larry; he (I) was just the one who'd gone public with them.

I called Janine that afternoon from a truck stop in Kansas and told her I'd gotten an emergency phone call from home that my grandmother was dying and I'd be in touch when I could. I asked her to call the bakery and video store and apologize for my lack of notice. She volunteered to fly out and meet me. She was so concerned, I felt bad about lying.

But not that bad.

Being with Beth again was like a shot of epinephrine plunged straight into the heart. The *Whoa!* I felt at her proximity was physical and exhilarating. Behind her blue eyes you could still see the wheels of her sharp mind clicking like tumblers in a safe. She threw away more ideas in an hour than most people got in a week.

If only she wasn't spending every spare minute making out with Simon.

This is what you get, I thought. You left without saying goodbye, you hurt her, she grieved for you, then moved on. Yet another voice emerged inside me, a more forceful one. *You're here now. So is she. Go for it.*

As the two of them continued to call each other pet

names, however, the possibility of hooking up with Beth grew more and more unlikely.[24]

But you know me; I love a long shot.

"We're going back to Boston." Beth drove as Simon sat beside her reading.

"I can't go home," I said.

"What are you talking about? Look at the state of the world. We need you."

"You can count me out of public life," I answered. "Been there, done that."

"There's a little more at stake now, don't you think?" Beth said. "We've had a war! The economy is in shambles! Besides, if I didn't think we needed you, I would have left you in Boulder contemplating the differences between relaxed and loose-fit jeans."

"That's not fair. I was at every peace rally in Boulder this year. I helped a congresswoman get elected. I got nine thousand names on a petition for better workers' rights." I thought I heard a snicker coming from Simon in the front seat.

"No, you're right—we just need to turn up the volume, that's all." Beth adjusted the rearview mirror and shot me what I hoped was an encouraging look.

How could Simon and his James Bond charm possibly compete with all the years of history Beth and I shared?[25] I leaned across the seat toward her.

---

[24]They used more animal terminology than I did back at C.U.

[25]Speaking of James Bond, is this car equipped with an ejection seat?

"I hope you're not thinking I'm going to come out and say it was all a hoax, that I never really died. If I did it for anyone, Beth, I'd do it for you. But I can't."

"Josh, give it a rest. You're being totally melodramatic."

"*You* give it a rest," I said. "You weren't the one being followed into the bathroom by paparazzi. You weren't the subject of a million tabloid stories."

"That's still no excuse for faking your own death," she said. "You were a coward, plain and simple."

She wasn't telling me anything I hadn't thought a thousand times already. But coming from her, the words felt like flaming cannonballs.

"Then let me out now." I was suddenly overcome by an avalanche of mistakes and missed opportunities. "I don't need to be kidnapped by someone who just wants to give me grief."

She sounded surprised. "Is that what you think? We're bringing you back because we need you."

"To do what?"

The way Simon coughed, I knew he was setting up for a sales pitch. "There's a state representative seat open in your district back home. We thought Larry might be a good candidate to run."

"Larry's dead." I turned to Beth. "That's your district too. Why don't *you* run?"

"If you say no, I will. But let's face it, Josh—we could never get as much press as we could with Larry. People all over the country are trying to break into politics on a grassroots level. You could really help."

"You have to be eighteen to run for state rep," I said. "My birthday's not till next September."

"Exactly. You'd be eighteen before the election. You should think about it, Josh."

"Absolutely not. Forget it."

"I'll run then. It's no big deal." She slipped her arm across the car to play with Simon's hair. If she was trying to torture me, she was succeeding.

After we stopped at a rest area to refuel, I lassoed Beth into the backseat with me. I imagined we were in a limousine where I could push the button that raised the dark glass between the front and back seats, eliminating Simon from our periphery. Instead, I mentally blocked him out and focused on Beth. I spotted her tattoo peeking out from the bottom of her pants—a dollar sign with a slash through it. She caught me looking at her.

"It's faded in the past few years." She seemed tired and restless. "I've been working non-stop forever. I feel like I've faded a little too."

I put my arm around her, ignoring Simon in the front seat.

"The changing-the-world business is tough," Beth said. "But I thought you might want to jump back in."

Those were the magic words, and Beth knew it. How many times had I uttered that phrase to Ms. Phillips in guidance, the standard answer for what I wanted to do with my life? *Change the world.* Did I still have the strength and determination to get it together and try to make a difference?

Was it my destiny, my vocation?

Or was I just trying to impress a girl?

As I looked at Beth, I wondered if the reason why even mattered.

. . .

We spent the night in a youth hostel; Beth settled into the women's wing while Simon and I shared a bunk at the other end of the hall. Considering I hadn't really packed, he was nice enough to let me borrow his toothpaste.

I tried not to focus on his habit of stroking his beard when he spoke; the thought of those fingers also touching Beth was disconcerting to say the least.

"Beth was hell-bent on finding you," Simon said. "She spent all her tuition money for this semester. Too bad she couldn't get course credit for all the time and effort she put in."

I told him I wasn't sure I was worth the trouble.

"Every activist we've spoken to has had a rough few years," he said. "So Beth got it in her head that if you were around, you'd come up with some new ideas." He looked me up and down. "Can't say I see what all the fuss was about."

I didn't disagree. Besides my work at PIRG, most of my energy had gone into studying flight or fight response in mammals.[26]

"I hate to let her down, but I don't know how much help I'd be." I sat next to him on the bunk. "There are so many problems in the world, I wouldn't know where to start."

---

[26]My vote now—flee.

"Well, you could start by making a difference in your home state."

Home. After being on the road for so long, it was more a concept than anything else.

Simon shut off his light and fell asleep quickly.[27] I sorted through what Beth had thrown in the box: laptop, textbook, notes. I had already planned on getting back to seventy-five possessions as my New Year's resolution; now it would be easy.

I skimmed my Word Search until I found a quote, this one from Martin Luther King Jr. *"Take the first step in faith. You don't have to see the whole staircase, just take the first step."* The time I'd spent as a political spectator lately made the thought of contributing seem overwhelming. Was it possible to take just *one* step, without walking off a ledge like last time? I shoved the papers back into my notebook and climbed to the top bunk.

I clicked on the light and took out my ethology textbook, envious of how simple and intuitive decisions could be in the animal world.

---

[27]He snored with an accent, I swear.

No matter where you turned on the radio, Christmas carols filled the air. Simon had the irritating habit of misinterpreting the lyrics and singing along with his own version of every song we heard. I let "Deck the Halls with Buddy Holly" slide, but when he sang "He's making a list, chicken and rice," I felt I had to step in.

"Simon, the mondegreens are killing me."[28]

"I know," Beth said. "Isn't it cute?"

"I was thinking more like lame."

"Simon, tell him about the first time you heard the Pledge of Allegiance."

He blushed, she laughed, they looked at each other adoringly. Why aren't cars equipped with barf bags?

Beth couldn't control her laughter. "He thought it said 'I led the pigeons toward the flag'!"

"I can see why you're so in love." Somebody kill me now.

Thankfully, Simon shut off the radio and we went back to discussing public policy. Tax rebates for the wealthy, continued

---

[28]Just because I was buying Tommy Hilfiger boxer shorts, you didn't think I gave up perusing the dictionary Web sites, did you?

strife in the Middle East, the increasing gap between poor and rich—there were plenty of topics to discuss.

What rankled us most was the way the average citizen viewed the political system. People felt used and manipulated by the whole process. I mean, did anyone believe in the "one person, one vote" theory anymore? On top of that, hardly anyone voted FOR a candidate; most voted for the lesser of two evils. Our democracy had been turned into a spectator sport while we sat around watching TV.[29] We lamented the fact that the fastest growing political party was the group of people who didn't vote at all.

Combined, the three of us had traveled thousands of miles around the world and had seen firsthand many of the issues that concerned us. But after the last Larry fiasco, I knew we needed more than words to make a difference.

When we reached the familiar exit of the Mass Pike, a more practical question concerned me: How could I possibly knock on the door of my old house and stand face-to-face with my stepfather? Would Peter hug me, glad I was still alive, then send me crashing through the wall? Would he do his famous pace-the-living-room-and-yell routine? Or maybe these worst-case scenarios were in my mind; maybe no one in the world cared one iota if I returned, including Peter.

"I can't do it," I told Beth. "I've hurt him too much. He doesn't deserve for this to re-surface again."

---

[29]Myself included. I still was trying to recover from months of *The Planet's Funniest Animals.*

She talked to me like a mother soothing a child. "Maybe things can be different now."

I'd read in some Larry-follow-up story a while ago that my stepfather had married Katherine, his Humpty-Dumpty-crazed girlfriend who had driven me out of my mind in the years since my mother's death. I couldn't deal with the thought of her answering the front door.

"Why don't we go to the woods for a while and just sit?" I suggested. "I'm not sure this is a good idea."

"Look," Beth said. "We'll drop you off. If you want to go in, fine. If you don't, we'll hook up with you later."

Simon threw in his unsolicited two cents. "Beth, you forgot to tell me Josh was such a baby."

She swatted his headrest hard enough to make him flinch. "This is serious stuff, Simon. Let it go."

The thing was—I felt like a baby. Felt like a boy who had just lobbed a baseball through the window of his neighbor's house and was walking up the front steps to apologize.[30] Like the imaginary boy who hit the ball, I deserved whatever punishment I got. Bring it on, Peter. I'm sorry.

"We'll be at my parents'," Beth said as they dropped me off. "Call me later, okay?"

I stood in front of my old house like a petrified tree. My hopes of Peter being out of town were shattered by the lights shining from the living room and kitchen. Was I ready to be

---

[30]This had never actually happened, of course. Baseball was too slow a game for me. (That and the fact that I couldn't hit the ball, no matter how many times at bat.)

Josh again? To take the heat for my actions? After several minutes, I took a deep breath and rang the doorbell.

The man who answered the door seemed like he was related to Peter—the same dark eyes, the same build—but with longish, graying hair and a twinkling smile. He was tan and wore a T-shirt and jeans. He let out a scream when he saw me. A delighted scream.

Only when he threw his arms around me did I realize it *was* Peter.

"I'm so sorry," I stammered. "I never should have left like that. . . ."

He wouldn't let go of me, just held me close. "God, Josh, it's good to see you."

I was embarrassed by his newfound enthusiasm. He finally let go, then held me at arm's length and looked me over. "I missed you, son."

The word detonated years of emotions inside me—hurt, loneliness, shame. I leaned against him and began to cry.

• • •

When we sat at the kitchen table to talk, I couldn't reconcile this open, smiling man with the one I'd lived with for years. I mean, the guy wore an *earring*. "You're so different," I said. "What happened?"

"I did a lot of soul-searching after you left, saw a lot of things I didn't like. I paint houses now—love it!"

I asked him where Katherine was.

"Didn't work out, lasted just three months." He told me

she'd moved to Boca Raton and opened a gift shop. "We still keep in touch. The shop's perfect for her, just perfect."

It seemed like Peter held no animosity toward anyone.

I felt it was my responsibility to tell him about that morning on the Sagamore Bridge, but when I started to speak, he held up his hand to stop me.

"I don't want to hear it. I read that book when it came out—couldn't tell if it was true or not. Decided if you were alive, my door would always be open." He motioned at the space between us. "Now is all that matters."

Since I'd left, Peter had gone from a capitalist robot to a Zen painter, and Beth had become a globe-trotting activist with an international boyfriend. What else had I missed?

"Are you staying for a while?" Peter asked. "I'd love to hang out with you."

I'd love to hang out with you. This from a guy who spent most of my high school years scheduling business trips during my school vacations so he wouldn't have to deal with me being home. I told him I was still undecided about being Josh again.

"Whatever you decide, I'm behind you 100 percent."

All this positive support began to give me a headache. I retreated to my old room.

The room was now set up as a kind of den, but my bed was still beside the window as if I'd never gone. In the closet, I found several boxes of the things I'd left behind. I picked up the statue of Ganesh and ran my fingers across the clay of the elephant's trunk. It suddenly seemed impossible to be in this house without my mother. A wave of grief almost knocked me into Peter's desk. Mom. I thought about her every day, of course, but being here now made me feel as if I could never get past the loss. I tore at the collar of my shirt. I ran outside for some air, hopped the backyard fence, and walked the well-worn path between my yard and Beth's. The Larsons' hedges were trimmed with snow and Christmas lights; I felt as if I were ten years old again.

She opened the sliding glass door with a smile. "Peter's a totally different guy, right?"

"Did they add something to the water here? If so, open the floodgates."

She threw on her jacket and sat on the cement steps with me.

"Where are your parents?" I asked.

"They're in Florida with Gram."

"And Sir Simon?"

"Doing an extra-credit paper for his political theory class."

"Of course he is." I exhaled and watched my breath escape in clouds of New England air. "I feel like everyone is moving forward except me."

She pulled me toward her. "It's your turn now."

I told her I wasn't sure where to begin. But as soon as the words left my mouth, I knew the statement was wrong. There were two places I needed to go before I could deal with the reality of being back in Boston, of being Josh again.

But for now, I decided to take Peter's advice and enjoy the moment. *This* moment of sitting on Beth's steps, gazing at the stars, and basking in the joy of finally coming home.

"Mom? Are you still here?"

I climbed onto the padded stool and waited.

The makeup counter at Bloomingdale's had been renovated since my last visit. The floors and lighting were different, but the same atmosphere of luxury and spending remained. Of the many places where I felt my mother's spirit, this makeup department was where I clearly heard her voice.

Marlene held her hand to her chest.[31] "Oh, my God, is that you, Joshie? But—"

When she finally overcame her shock, she reached across the counter for a hug. I gave her a quick recap of what had happened then made her swear not to tell a soul.

"Honey, honey, it's so good to see you." She held up my face to the lights. "But you're so dehydrated!"

I told her I'd been doing a lot of hiking.

"Without moisturizing?" She grabbed a jar from the shelf and applied the cream to my cheeks in tiny circles. I smiled in

---

[31]When I was a kid, I used to pretend her penciled-in eyebrows were connected to her mouth like marionette strings, making her talk.

spite of myself. Sometimes there was nothing more comforting than the predictable, even for a hyperactive guy like me.

"I was thinking about your mother the other day—God rest her soul. She would've loved the new burgundy line." Marlene adjusted her glasses then looked at me approvingly. "You want me to leave for a few minutes?"

"Do you mind?"

"Not at all, honey. Holiday traffic today—you should get lucky." She high-tailed it over to a woman dripping cash on the other side of the counter.

I closed my eyes and settled into the chair. Most people sat on this stool for makeovers; I suppose in some strange way, I did too. I'd been to several Bloomingdale's in my travels, sat at other makeup counters, but never heard my mother speak to me anywhere but here in Chestnut Hill.

The silence was deafening. Had I lost my ability to hear her? Had her spirit relocated in the past few years without leaving me a forwarding address?

"Come on, Mom," I muttered. "Talk to me."

People walked by in droves, too busy consuming to speak. Marlene circled by as she rang up the woman's purchase.

"Any luck?"

I shook my head. This is what you get, I thought. This is the price for living a disconnected life, for not sticking to your path. You can't hear her anymore. I waited a few more minutes before leaving, too upset to even say goodbye to Marlene.

As I left the department, a woman bent down next to her

toddler son who was trying to fasten his Velcro boots. "Try again, sweetie. Don't give up."

I almost yelped with joy. A faded connection perhaps, but a beginning.

Outside, I unlocked my bike from the tree and pedaled to the day's second destination, almost giddy with anticipation.

It was the perfect day to begin a vision quest.[32]

It took me the rest of the day to dig out the hole. Years of neglect had left the bottom of my old hideaway full of soggy leaves and branches. But the physical work exhilarated me. When I returned home to grab provisions and a shower, Peter asked if he could do anything to help. I told him I was in the process of working things out for myself.

• • •

Early the next morning, I took food and water for several days. I told Peter I'd see him when I returned; he wished me luck. (I needed a vision quest just to get used to the new Peter.)

Inside the hole, I wrapped my down sleeping bag tightly around me. I'd missed it here, missed the smell of the damp earth and the unpredictability of the weather. I tried to empty my mind enough to begin the task at hand. I thought about Janine, wondering if she had tried to get ahold of me in Chicago. I'd call her when I got back home; she deserved a truthful explanation.

---

[32]Okay, it wasn't perfect—it was thirty-four degrees. A short, cold vision quest.

When I got back around to the topic at hand, I knew Beth was right—it was time for me to contribute again. I needed to add my voice to those commenting on the culture, to be connected to what was vital and meaningful in our lives. The part of me that studied and outlined information told me to pick one issue and dedicate myself to it. But the part of me that enjoyed ten projects at once wanted to multi-task my way across everything in our society that needed addressing.

The question remained—*how?* Was politics the answer? The local representative seat?

My mind clicked from one thought to the next. When I was traveling through the country incognito,[33] the emotion I felt most often was fear—of getting caught or being recognized. I can say firsthand that living in constant fear is one of the most unproductive, life-draining states of mind there is. What I noticed now that I had uninterrupted time to think was that the rest of the country was living in fear too. The headlines were full of one horrifying piece of news after another. War, cutbacks, terrorism, states of alert, secret government meetings, citizens' rights being violated—the list went on and on. How had we gone from a country of peace and prosperity to one of such deep-rooted anxiety and panic? Were these feelings warranted, or was our government bombarding us with so much horrible news that no one dared question its authority? How much of this fear was justified, and how much was being sold? When you spent as much time in nature as I did, all the

---

[33] I love that word.

42

news and terror seemed manufactured, not real. The world I inhabited was amazing and bountiful. Was it possible for a handful of people to break through the clouds of fearful rhetoric to expose the beautiful and abundant? Sitting in this hole deep in the woods where the transcendentalist movement began, I felt like the national psyche had been hijacked by a wayward boogeyman.

And for someone my age, the threats were greater. I would be eighteen soon, eligible for the draft if it was ever reinstated. I didn't want to go to war—ever. Spend days and nights trying to kill other guys my age? No thanks. The longer I sat in the darkness, the more I realized how necessary it was to get deeply involved in what was going on in this country.

On my second day, I was feeling punch-drunk and cold and almost didn't hear the voice calling me from the top of the hole.

"Josh?"

"Beth? What are you doing here?"

By the time she slid down into my hideout, her clothes were covered in leaves and snow.

"How long have you known about this place?" I asked.

"I used to come here to hike after you died.[34] I found this hole one day and just knew you had made it."

"I think you should forget Brown and go into the private-eye business."

---

[34]It was the wrong choice of words, but I knew what she meant.

She looked up at me, her hair full of tiny bits of bark. "Do you want me to leave?"

"No, but you're probably the only person I'd let interrupt a vision quest. I'm getting a lot of good thinking done."

"I just want you to know I'm committed to Simon."

I didn't know what to say to such a non sequitur.

She pulled her jacket over her head. "But I think we have some unfinished business, don't you?"

Okay, I thought. You're definitely hallucinating. Two days in the cold with just water, trail mix, and gum, searching for the true meaning of life, and this is what you get. A mirage. Shake it off.

But when she pressed her body against me, the reality of the situation struck like lightning.

It took me about half a second to respond.

I back-burnered my save-the-world questions and decided to make one of my own dreams come true.

Beth told me later that what we had done didn't change anything, that we had important work to do, that she was serious about Simon . . . blah, blah, blah.

But everything had changed.

I don't want you to think I reverted to some dopey guy following Beth around like a puppy. I was cool, gave her a boost up out of the hole after the rain stopped, waved goodbye with a smile.

You know when you finally do something you've been obsessed with for years, and somehow afterward it feels anticlimactic, not worthy of all the hype?

This wasn't one of those times.

The term "slow-motion" doesn't begin to describe the care I took in playing back my afternoon with Beth. Her kissing my chest, my muddy hands pulling her toward me, the sky opening up and pouring down on us afterward.

It was messy.

It was beautiful.

It ruined my vision quest.

I went home and ate a three-egg omelet with half a jar of salsa, then took the longest, hottest shower of my life.

I had been happy with Janine—she was kind and gregarious and fun—but this was *Beth*. As for Simon? I didn't care what Beth said about her commitment to him. His reign was over.

I wanted to play it cool,[35] so I didn't rush over to Beth's. I grabbed a notebook and a handful of markers and headed for the basement.

In the cocoon-like safety of my swing, I outlined several ideas. I got so carried away mapping out various projects, I ran out of paper in the first fifteen minutes.

I left the swing for the larger space of the workroom. Cans of paint lined the walls, probably leftovers from Peter's jobs. I rolled out a giant drop cloth until it covered most of the basement floor. I took a brush from the tray next to the sink and began graphing my thoughts. Soon the tarp looked like an abstract expressionist painting with chunks of color representing possible avenues of action.[36]

When it was dark, I took a break and cleaned up. Peter had left a message saying he was in Worcester and wouldn't be home until tomorrow. So I figured enough time had passed for a non-desperate visit to Beth's.

In all the turmoil of coming home, I hadn't made Beth a Christmas present. She and I had always celebrated the holidays as non-materialistically as possible—we made each other presents. So I sat down and spilled my guts in a letter,

---

[35]For once.
[36]I may not solve any of society's problems, but I was certainly enjoying myself.

detailing how I'd felt about her for years and the new level we'd taken the relationship to. The thing was mushier than a stupid pop song, but the words just wouldn't stop. I took the Ganesh statue from its box in the closet and wrapped it carefully in one of my T-shirts. I headed over to her house.

But what I saw from the edge of her yard froze me in my steps.

She and Simon were making snow angels.

They were lying on their backs, holding hands, and naming the constellations. *Our* constellations, the ones Beth and I had named a hundred times before.

But the most painful part of watching Beth and Simon? They looked *happy*.

I'd witnessed Beth with Todd, with Charlie, with Dave—but never this relaxed and comfortable with someone else.

She was right about one thing she'd said earlier today: Nothing had changed between us. Nothing at all.

I shoved the letter in my pocket and trudged home.

I tried to hate her—for using me, playing with my mind, cheating on him—but I couldn't muster up the anger. Whatever she did to me from here on in was nothing compared to what I'd put her through. She had me over a barrel and she knew it.

I hurried to the basement to put my pent-up energy to use. But this time, the paint splattered and flew across the tarp at warp speed. Where my work that afternoon had been meticulous and well thought out, this was wild and raw. A Pollock of pain.

Should I go back to Boulder? Hit the road? Come out of hiding and be Larry? Work side by side with Beth and Simon? Oh, and by the way—Happy New Year!

I picked up the phone and called Janine, but all I got was her answering machine with the *Banana Splits* theme song. I wanted to tell her that my name wasn't Mark, that I was in love with someone else, but that I still thought about her all the time. Instead, I quietly dropped the phone back into its base. Josh Swensen—King of Calling Old Girlfriends and Hanging Up. I barely slept.

I woke up at three, full of anxiety. It took me a few minutes to realize why. Between the pre-dawn darkness and Peter's absence, it was almost exactly like the morning I'd left two years ago. I washed up quickly, grabbed Peter's bike this time, and headed into the early morning.

My body knew where I was going long before my mind acknowledged it. Hour after hour, I pedaled south, then east. Thankfully, most of the roads were clear.

Somewhere around Plymouth, I couldn't avoid facing my destination.

I was returning to the scene of the crime.

As I pedaled, the colors and lines I'd painted yesterday congealed into some kind of plan. The task this time seemed Herculean—or was it quixotic?[37] That was also what made it appealing.

Once I hit Wareham, I coasted—almost afraid to catch a

---

[37]To throw in some references from Ms. Kelly's senior year lit class.

glimpse of the bridge. I stopped at a diner to use the bathroom and down two bagels and a bottle of water. Should I go along with Simon and Beth's idea or follow my own path? I wrote down my idea on the napkin in front of me. Was I being too delusional this time, even for me? No, delusional was thinking I could ever end up with Beth. *This* idea seemed almost attainable compared to that one. I told myself to quit stalling, got back on the bike, and headed toward the Sagamore.

As I pedaled across the bridge, my body instinctively pulled over to the same spot I'd stopped at back then. It was much less windy than that previous day, but no less threatening. I leaned my bike against the stanchion and gazed over the side.

How had I even *pretended* to jump? My hands clenched the girder for support. I felt as dizzy and nauseous as I had the morning of my pseudocide. Stand here, I thought. Stand here until you realize what you've done. What you're going to do.

I looked across the bay and let the past few years flash before me—the campsites, the hostels, the lies, the fake IDs, the paranoia, the loneliness. Yes, I had met interesting people and traveled to parts of the country I never would have seen otherwise. But I'd traveled as an interloper, a fugitive.

The wind pressed against my back, pinning me to the railing. I let myself feel the isolation of my existence. This wasn't about Beth, my mother, Peter, or even Janine; it was about me. I didn't know what the future held, where my place was in the universal plan, but I did know this.

I didn't want to be Mark anymore. Or Carl or Gil or Tom.

Whatever the future held, I would meet my fate as Josh Swensen. And that meant embracing Larry again. And being Larry meant contributing in a big way. I unfolded the napkin I'd scribbled on in the diner and read my New Year's resolution.

This year I will run for president.

I couldn't *be* president, of course; no one my age could. The Constitution was quite clear that you had to be thirty-five to serve. But there was nothing in that document that said I couldn't raise issues or voice my opinion.

Absurd?

You bet.

But that was what drew me to the idea.

A police car pulled alongside me, lights flashing. The cop in the passenger seat got out of the car cautiously and asked if there was a problem.

I shook my head and looked past him to the dark water below. "Don't worry, I'm not thinking about jumping."[38]

I thought about turning myself in, throwing my bike in their trunk and hitching a ride toward my newly decided fate. Instead, I hopped on my bike and headed toward Boston.

I had a lot of work to do.

---

[38]This time.

PART TWO

"The future will not belong to those who are content with the present. The future will not belong to cynics and people who sit on the sidelines. The future will belong to people who have passion and are willing to work hard to make this country better."

Senator Paul Wellstone

ELECTION COUNTDOWN
JANUARY:
SET UP STRATEGY

The next several days showcased me at my best: locking myself in my room and working. I ran Internet searches and pored through data, made calculations, and created action plans. I was thankful Peter honored my request for privacy.

Beth came by several times, but I ignored her.

"You're being immature!" she said through my barricade. "Let's talk about what happened."

"I've got more important things on my mind," I answered.

She would storm off and return several hours later.

I continued to dissect our political system for the next five days. When Beth came by on Sunday, I unlocked the door when she knocked.

"Well, it's about time." She entered my room and plopped on the bed. "Are you trying to invent sticky-note wallpaper? You can't even find the windows in here."

"It's all categorized—don't touch anything."

"About the other day," she began. "I used bad judgment. It was a mistake."

"Was it?" I wasn't going to budge on this one.

"Do you think it was?" she asked.

"Do you?"

"I didn't until you locked yourself in your room for a week."

"You think I've been in here obsessing about *you*?" I loved having the upper hand with her—for a change. "I've been setting up the groundwork for my next project."

She bounced on the bed with enthusiasm. "Are you going to make a comeback? Run for the state rep seat?"

"I've decided to push the envelope a little farther this time."

"Josh, this is great. Wait till I tell—"

"Duckie?"

She swatted me in the arm. "I *knew* he bothered you. I knew it!"

I inched closer to her on the bed. "I've been doing a lot of thinking these past few days, and I want to ask you something."

She didn't back away from me. "Sure."

I leaned in toward her, close to her ear. "Will you be my running mate?"

Her puzzled expression was priceless.

I described my plan in detail, answering her questions with plausible explanations. "Come on, it'll be fun."

"When we talked about resurrecting Larry, we were thinking more in terms of the publicity and media attention," she said. "We never thought of taking it so wide—"

"Yeah, well, maybe Simon just doesn't have enough vision."

She got up from the bed and headed toward the door. "That's what this is all about, isn't it? Pissing off Simon?"

I pointed to the hundreds of sticky notes plastered around my room. "Yeah, this is all about Simon. Give me a break."

She didn't say goodbye, just bolted from the room. But from my vantage point,[39] I watched her pace through my yard for twenty minutes. I dashed back to my room as she re-entered the house.

"Okay," she said. "But we're partners. We make every decision equally, no lying like last time."

"Deal."

"One more thing." She pulled herself up to her full height, just a few inches shorter than my own. "I'm with Simon. This is *not* up for negotiation. Whatever happened, happened."

"Or whatever happens, happens."

She looked at me in anger, then smiled when she saw I was laughing. "We're going to do this," she said. "Really blow this old, rich white man thing apart."

When I kissed her, she didn't stop me.

"I've got to admit," she said when we came up for air, "you do have the best ideas."

"The Wizard, at your service."

"Oh my God, I have to call my adviser and arrange to take more time off. And Simon! He'll have a million suggestions." She gave me a squeeze and left.

As much as I tried not to wonder what Simon would think of my plan, his opinion did matter. I opened the kitchen window to hear something, anything, but nothing came.

I drove to the old Victorian downtown that Peter was help-ing to renovate and told him the news.

---

[39]Standing on a stool in the downstairs bathtub.

"President of what?" he asked.

"Uhm, the United States?"

"But—"

"I know I can't *really* run, but there are so many issues I want to call attention to."

He started laughing. "I didn't know you were interested in a political career."

"I'm not really, just interested in change."

He nodded without speaking.

"This isn't one of my phases," I said. "Not like when I was obsessed with being the next Mel Blanc. I'm going to follow through on this one."

"Till the Board of Elections puts the kibosh on the whole thing."

"I've got some ideas on that. But first—will you be my campaign manager?"

He almost dropped his can of semi-gloss. "Josh, I don't know what to say. All those years we—"

"Hated each other?" I suddenly flipped back into the interrupting, argumentative kid I'd always been with him.

"We did hate each other, didn't we? Such a waste of time." He told me to count him in, but we'd have to talk later because he had only a few hours of daylight left to finish up the trim. My new campaign manager then wiped his brow and headed back to his ladder.

• • •

Beth, Simon, and I worked through the afternoon and evening. Besides the snow angel episode, I hadn't seen Simon since Beth had visited me on my vision quest. When she left to get the adaptor for her laptop, he walked over to the window.

"You can stop smirking," Simon said. "I know all about you and Beth."

"What are you talking about?" I asked.

"She told me everything."

"She told you about *us*?"

"Down to the last muddy details. It's fine. Don't worry about it."

"She *told* you?"

Simon shrugged. "On to more important matters, yes?"

MORE IMPORTANT MATTERS? While Simon outlined his campaign ideas, I thought about his casual attitude toward Beth and his no-need-to-worry attitude about me. Even with that amazing afternoon with his girlfriend, I was obviously not considered much of a threat.

But it was hard to hate the guy; he worked hours as long as I did, was passionate and committed to change. He had been home-schooled, tutored by Oxford graduate students, and already held three patents.[40] I had no choice but to bond with him; we needed his input.

---

[40]Thermodynamic propulsion devices. I love science, but I still had to run for my old textbooks after Simon left.

Besides, he loved Monty Python. And when Beth walked in on Simon and me doing the cheese shop routine, she looked at us both with such equal affection, it almost didn't matter that she went home with him.[41]

. . .

The first thing I had to do was rise from the dead. My mind raced through several scenarios from staging a revisionist re-enactment of the Resurrection to taking out a full-page ad in the *Globe*. In the end, I went with the mundane choice of holding a press conference.

I tried to call Janine to tell her before I went public, but she must've still been in Seattle visiting her parents for the holidays.[42] My e-mails to her went unanswered.

Peter called the various local and national media, stating he had news about his stepson who had been presumed dead. It didn't take long for the newspapers to comb their archives for news first on my "capture" by betagold, then on my "death." Once they realized the potential story, they raced to the house for the 4 P.M. conference.

From the safety of my room, I watched the all-too-familiar phalanx of television equipment fill the street and came down with a serious case of flop sweat.

"This was a giant mistake," I told Beth.

"It stinks, but after this we can concentrate on the campaign."

_____

[41]Almost.

[42]Or come to her senses and realized what a fake I was.

I pointed to the reporters descending on the front lawn. "They don't want to hear me talk about issues. They just want the dirt on my 'death.'"

"They don't want to hear *anyone* talk about issues. They'd rather write about you dashing across the country like that guy in *The Fugitive*."

Peter entered the room, a ringmaster about to take the stage. He wore a hand-scrawled LARRY FOR PRESIDENT T-shirt he'd painted that morning. "How're you holding up, Josh?"

"Not well."

"You want to change your mind, you can."

He and Beth looked at me expectantly. "Let's get this over with," I said.

When I walked out the front door, the whir of the shutters and videocameras sounded like the clicking lock on a door being closed. I suppose there are many kids who dream about this kind of fame, but it's a whole lot different from the inside, believe me.

I read from my prepared statement—that the media glare had driven me to extreme measures, that I regretted the pain I'd caused my friends and family, etc., etc., etc. It began to dawn on me why I had hidden behind a screen name in the first place. I'm not someone who normally spends a lot of time worrying about getting rejected—because I've had so much practice—but I could actually feel the crowd scrutinize every word from my mouth. I was forced to muster all the persistence I had to finish my statement without heading for my hole in the woods mid-sentence. I was bombarded with questions: Was my pseudocide pre-meditated? Had I committed fraud?[43] Was I starting up the Web site again? I finally got around to why we were all there.

Politicians assume young men and women of my genera-
tion are too apathetic to actually stop them from looting
the world's cookie jars, but they are wrong. There are mil-
lions of young people in this country who are sick to death
of suits running the show with a blatant disregard for the
price future generations will have to pay for their greedi-
ness and arrogance. You may not realize this, but we are
part of the backbone of this country. We're the ones who
make your coffees, serve your food, clean your houses,
watch your kids. And what do we get in return? Wages so
low we have to work two jobs, with no health care, no ben-
efits. In what kind of universe does that make sense?
We're only important to you as consumers, when we're
spending our hard-earned money on your STUFF. This is
OUR country too—we deserve a say in things.

The late Senator Paul Wellstone once said, "Let there
be no distance between the words you say and the life
you live." I, for one, am ready to put my time and effort
where my mouth is.

---

[43]Because I wasn't insured, Peter hadn't filed any claim after my death, so there was no fraud. And because I didn't leave a note, there was no way to prove I had planned a suicide anyway. Peter got his attorney involved to ensure that my answers were worded correctly. As I explained to both of them, my original plan had been to return quickly after the furor died down. Unfortunately, news of my "death" had only fueled the fire.

I know at my age it's impossible for me to serve as president of the United States,[44] but I'm tossing my hat into the ring to raise the many issues young people have with the way this country's goodwill and natural resources are being exploited into extinction. Our leaders are supposed to work for US; they should be doing what WE want them to do, not the other way around.

As much as I hate the thought of being back in the public eye, I can't sit in the comfort of my privacy and hope that other people will address these issues. That is why I am declaring my candidacy for president of the United States of America. I will run as the candidate from the PEACE PARTY, an independent third party we announce today.

I introduced Beth as my running mate and told the reporters we'd be announcing our campaign schedule within the week.

I asked if there were any questions. Big mistake.

A man in a dark blue suit smiled politely. "You disappeared for two years, right? Pretended you were dead? How can you possibly think that's the kind of person this country wants in the White House? How can you be trusted?"

Before I could answer, someone else chimed in. "Don't you think we need someone who takes his responsibilities seriously?"

---

[44]Here's where the cameras clicked into overdrive.

"Someone who *has* responsibilities," a woman added. "Do you even have a job?"

I told her that, believe it or not, running for president would be a full-time commitment.

"But before that, did you work?"

"I've worked lots of jobs all across the country. My last positions were assistant baker and videostore clerk."

Outright laughter.

"You probably live at home," the woman continued. "With your stepfather paying the expenses."

"Yes, but—"

A man aggressively stuck a microphone in my face. "I'd like to know how you have the audacity to talk about something as important as voting when you've probably never voted yourself."

I tried to remain calm. "Good question. I'm turning eighteen this year, and voting is something I can't wait to do."

"This is a sick joke," another reporter said. "You're criticizing our government when the chances are *zero* that someone with your level of experience has anything to offer the people of this country at all."

"These are all good points," I said. "I'll be talking about them at length in my campaign."

The crowd descended on me like a pack of hyenas. I had expected skepticism, sure, but this was all-out anger. Had I miscalculated that much?

"I'm not saying I'm the best person for the job," I said. "And I certainly don't have instant answers. I'm just saying the issues of ordinary citizens—especially our youth—are not being addressed."

Simon gave me the high sign, then pulled me inside. Peter stayed on the lawn answering more questions. By the time everyone left, I felt like I'd been stuck on the spin cycle of a runaway washing machine. Even I had doubts about the long-term wisdom of my idea.

"Well, that went well." Beth covered her face with a pillow from the couch and screamed.

"Luckily there wasn't any produce around," Simon added.

"Am I nuts?" I asked. "They'll turn the pseudocide into a character issue, they'll make it look like I did something bad."

The three of them stared at me mutely.

"Okay, it *was* kind of bad. But the guy's right—I've never even voted!"

"You *can't* vote," Beth argued. "It's not your fault."

"This was stupid," I said.

Simon literally pulled me out of the chair. "We're going downstairs and having our strategy meeting. A few lousy reporters are not going to derail us. We'll be facing much bigger obstacles than that."

I hated him for it, but he was right. I grabbed my notes and headed to the basement.

• • •

I'd spent the week studying the last several reports from the U.S. Census Bureau and had come up with a formula for the perfect administration. Our campaign staff—and Cabinet, if we could've gotten elected—would mirror the general population as reflected in the reports. Simon and I raced to calculate the final numbers.[45] We labeled the document "The Peace Party Mission Statement" and posted it on the Larry Web site.

I also insisted we use our first names to run. Based on the concept of "We Work for You, Not the Other Way Around," it seemed appropriate to call the ticket Larry / Beth instead of Swensen / Coleman. I wrote our names on a sticky note and added it to the hundreds of others on my wall.

The story made it to the *Boston Globe* and the *New York Times* the next day. Both papers treated my candidacy as a joke. I decided to make a few local appearances to gauge the average person's reaction. If the idea of running for president wasn't worth pursuing, we'd come up with Plan B.

Some news outlets did call, but Beth was right. No one wanted to hear our thoughts on consumerism, hunger, or poverty. One after another, the reporters asked about where I'd slept on the road, if betagold had tried to find me, if I'd had any romantic liaisons in my travels. It was embarrassing; it was unimportant. I gave staccato answers, then steered the conversation toward more meaningful topics.

We had much better luck with the Web site.

I wasn't sure what kind of response to expect from the Internet; many of my fellow pilgrims from a few years ago

---

[45]Thankfully for my shattered ego, I beat him by several minutes.

might have moved on and forgotten about my message completely.

In the first twenty-four hours, we logged in more than thirty-five hundred hits.

Forty-three people volunteered to help with the campaign.

We were in business.

AMERICA'S YOUTH

THE TOBACCO INDUSTRY SPENDS $26 MILLION A DAY TO MARKET THEIR PRODUCTS WITH MANY OF THEIR EFFORTS DIRECTED TO KIDS.

ONE IN 145 U.S. CHILDREN DIE BEFORE THEIR FIRST BIRTHDAY.

EVERY 5.3 MINUTES, A CHILD IN THIS COUNTRY IS ARRESTED FOR A VIOLENT CRIME. WHY IS OUR CULTURE SO VIOLENT?

IN THE WARS OF THE LAST DECADE MORE CHILDREN WERE KILLED THAN SOLDIERS.

THE U.S. RANKS FIRST IN TECHNOLOGY, DEFENSE SPENDING, AND MILITARY SPENDING; LAST IN PROTECTING KIDS FROM GUN VIOLENCE.

MORE AMERICANS BETWEEN THE AGES OF 15 AND 24 ARE KILLED BY GUNS THAN BY ALL NATURAL CAUSES COMBINED.

A PERSON UNDER THE AGE OF 25 DIES FROM HIV EVERY DAY.

EVERY MINUTE, A BABY IN THE U.S. IS BORN WITHOUT HEALTH INSURANCE.

ONE IN 3 U.S. CHILDREN IS POOR AT SOME POINT DURING CHILDHOOD.

Op-ed pieces sprouted up in several newspapers: A seven-teen-year-old can't run for president! He's wasting valuable resources on a pie-in-the-sky campaign! He's trivializing the process! Peter and I had waged a bet on how long it would take before we were visited by one of many government agencies. I won; it took less than forty-eight hours.

The man introduced himself as Doug Graham, general counsel for the Massachusetts secretary of the common-wealth's office. He said he was concerned about my eligibility requirements.

He flipped through his notebook like a cop. "Non-party candidates need ten thousand signatures to run for president. You also need the signatures of twelve electors on your nomination papers. But most important, you don't meet the age requirement."

"I know. But after studying all the documents, it seems to me that I need to be thirty-five to *serve*, not to run."

"You need to be thirty-five to be on the ballot. That's where our office comes in." He explained that the secretary of the commonwealth's office served as a watchdog over the election, and they couldn't allow my name to be listed.

Peter's negotiation skills re-surfaced as he argued with the guy point for point.

"I actually thought this might happen," I interrupted. "There haven't been any precedents,[46] so I knew you'd be scurrying around trying to find a way to stop me from running."

"Not trying to stop you, just trying to follow the law."

"In that case, I'll be a write-in."

He told me there were laws for write-in candidates too, that they didn't even tally the results for a particular candidate unless he or she received more than 4 percent of the vote. "Four percent might sound insignificant, but that's more than eight million votes."

"I don't care about my name on the ballot; I just want at least *one* candidate to be focused on solving problems instead of fund-raising."

He shook my hand and wished me luck.

Peter and I moved to the next item on our agenda: finding a campaign headquarters.

On one of his painting jobs, Peter had met a local businessman whose run-down theater was tied up in divorce proceedings with his wife. Its worn velvet seats, hardwood stage, and kitchen in the back made the theater ideal for our

---

[46]Precedent, president, precedent, president—I love that.

purposes.[47] The owner said we could use the space until he could find a buyer or his wife got permission to knock it down, whichever came first. We happily set up office.

"Now, I don't want you to take this the wrong way," Peter said. "But I need you to hear me out."

I knew things between us had been going too smoothly.

"It's just that running a national campaign costs money, lots of money. I can understand you want to keep within the federal election spending limits—and I respect that, I really do."

I waited for the other shoe to drop.

"Problem is, the other candidates don't share your view that campaign financing is one of the biggest problems in Washington. They're taking donations hand over fist. How do we compete with that?"

"I refuse to take a penny from any PACs."[48]

"No offense, Josh, but those guys aren't going to give you money anyway."

"Good, because our money will come from somewhere else."

"Such as . . . ?"

"Do you know how many people in this country are between the ages of thirteen and nineteen?"

---

[47]My initial thought was to set up headquarters at my hole in the woods or as close to Walden Pond as we could get. I quickly nixed that plan when I realized I'd have absolutely nowhere left to go when I wanted to be alone.

[48]Political Action Committees—representing Big Business. They give a ton of money, but expect a lot in return—mostly legislation that benefits them.

"Of course I know. That's the market every company tries to target. About twenty-eight million."

"Right. And if you get half of them—" ·

"You'll never get half. You've got to use a more reasonable percentage."

"Okay, 10 percent."

"Still high, but better."

"If you get 10 percent of twenty-eight million kids to send you just five dollars, you've got fourteen million dollars to run a campaign."

"The last president spent $186 million to get elected."

"He didn't get elected; he got *selected*. And that $186 million doesn't count the $250 million of soft money Republicans funneled through the states to bypass federal laws. His opponent was no better; he spent $120 million with the Democrats raising another $220 million of soft money."

Peter whistled through his teeth. "That's almost a *billion* dollars! And some people still think it's not about the money."[49]

"Let's face it," I said. "Most politicians spend half their time raising money and the other half putting loopholes in their legislation to benefit contributors. I think there's something honorable about running a campaign financed with rolls of pennies and dollar bills sent in cards."

"It worked for Oprah," Peter said. "She's raised lots of money for charity that way."

---

[49]Forty-three percent of the incoming freshmen elected to Congress in 2002 were millionaires—just regular folks like us. According to my calculations, the candidates who spend the most money on their campaigns win 95 percent of the time.

"Pennies for a President."

"Spare Change for Sure Change."

I turned to him and laughed. "Hey, you're pretty good at this."

"Guess I haven't lost all the old skills."

When I noticed his voice catch, I asked him if he ever missed those days. He thought for several minutes before he answered.

"I miss some parts of my old life, I guess. Your mom and being good at my job. And I certainly miss that paycheck at the end of the month. But I feel more connected to my life now."

I came clean and told Peter about my consumer binge back in Boulder.

He laughed for several minutes. "Glad to know you are as flawed as the rest of us."

"Are you kidding? Half the time I feel like that's all I am."

"Join the club."

The two of us sat on those worn theater seats for the next two hours. By the time we went home I finally understood the meaning of the word "father."

ELECTION COUNTDOWN

MID-JANUARY:

RALLIES

We held our first campaign rally on the banks of Boston Harbor, mere steps from the site of the infamous Boston Tea Party, the country's original act of political theater. I wore a Native American headdress the same way some of the colonists had dressed up as Mohawks that fateful night. Two hundred and thirty years later, I was ready to toss some verbal cargo of my own. If only there had been more than twenty people there.

Call the Mad Hatter—We Need Another Tea Party!

Back in 1773, the British East India Company complained that they were suffering economic hardship, so the British government passed the Tea Act of 1773, letting them off the hook for paying taxes. The colonists of New England were furious that the government had given the company unfair advantage over smaller and local competitors. So they boycotted, eventually staging the historic Boston Tea Party on this very spot, an act that demonstrated they were tired of a government that favored Big Business over its own citizens. I say that the situation we citizens face today isn't much better than what our ancestors faced in our country's infancy. In fact, it's much worse.

Do you know that 83 percent of the government's income comes from people like you and me, and only 17 percent from corporations? Not so long ago, it used to be a fifty-fifty split. Why so unfair to the average citizen now? Because you and I don't have lobbyists fighting for our rights in Washington the way corporations do. Our politicians have taken so much money from Big Business for their campaign war chests that they have to listen to their concerns. They'll pay you and me lots of lip service, saying they care about our needs, but until we fork over the same kind of cash the corporations do, we're out of luck. As it is now, we go to our jobs every day so we can donate money to bail out the airlines, the banks, and the utilities. Our ancestors at the Tea Party rebelled over a whole lot less than that.

The Boston Tea Party was famous for another reason too—the tea boycott that followed was one of the earliest efforts where women in this country organized to change public policy. I'm happy to say my running mate, Beth Coleman, embodies the spirit of these brave and resourceful women. I invite all women and men, boys and girls, to work with us in effecting positive change again today. Those colonists went down in history for standing up against a government that valued corporations more than its own people; work with us now to stand up to this corporate-loving government again.

I wanted to toss a box of Lipton into the harbor as a grand finale but couldn't bring myself to litter.

By the time I'd finished, the crowd had doubled and there was actually a line at the voter registration table.

Beth was ecstatic. "Nice touch—adding in the piece about the women. They barely teach that part in school."

"Or the fact that the boycott got the nation off tea."

"Yeah, Starbucks has a lot to thank those women for."

We smiled at each other, our regular rhythm re-established.[50]

Afterward, we answered questions from dozens of people who lingered at the rally. Many were as concerned as I was about the minority of the rich absconding with the blueprint for our future. I had told myself that if I tanked at that first rally, I would rethink the campaign entirely. But that afternoon assured me that we were on the right track. Forget the naysayers, we were moving forward.

That is, until I saw the papers the next day.

Even with a group of interested people and our theatrics, there wasn't one mention in the *Globe* or *Herald*. If you hadn't read our Web site, you'd never know the rally had happened at all. I found myself in the strange position of actually *needing* the media this time around. And as anyone who's tried to swim against the corporate tide knows, the media's not in any hurry to bite the hand that feeds it.

---

[50]Does this mean you'll be cheating on Simon anytime soon?

I knew going into this that the press and current political system wouldn't make it easy for a seventeen-year-old to run for president. I just didn't think they'd make it impossible.

Still, kids continued to arrive at headquarters. Locals, then students from all across the country. Some wanted experience for their resumés, some a sense of political community. Most were in school, so we handed out assignments they could complete from home—making phone calls, staging local rallies. We held interviews for top field positions based on the demographics we'd set forth in our mission statement.

· · ·

Lisa, our new communications director, lived in Back Bay. At five feet ten inches, with her long blond hair pulled messily on top of her head and her ASK ME ABOUT BEING A DYKE T-shirt, she was stunning. She'd worked on several local campaigns and couldn't wait to roll up her sleeves on ours.

She leaned back and put her bare feet on the chair in front of her. "Okay, best case, we would've been doing groundwork a few years ago. Most campaigns aren't run this seat-of-the-pants."

"I know."

"But there's also something to be said about improvising, being able to make changes quickly as you go along."

"I'm with you."

"First thing: The Republicans and Democrats aren't going to waste any time with us at all. They think anyone this age can't be serious; they'll pretend we're not even here."

"Age is the best thing we have going for us," I said.

"Most people are going to think being seventeen—"

"I turn eighteen this year."

"Most people will link that to inexperience."

"Yes, but most people our age don't vote! Of the almost 27 million people between the ages of eighteen and twenty-four, only 32 percent made it to the polls last time!"

She readjusted her messy curls. "It's criminal."

"It's more than criminal. *We* could have changed the result of the last election. It was that close! If just a few more kids had voted, we could have altered history."

"Neither candidate addressed any issues kids care about," Lisa said. "They went to schools and *pretended* to care."

I jumped out of my seat. "The fact that we can't win is our strength, not our weakness. We have no lobbyists to piss off, no sponsors to keep happy. We're free to say what we think, unlike everyone else in this campaign."

"So turn it around on them?"

"Hell, yeah. Let's expose this dog and pony show for what it is." The ideas streamed from me unedited. "Let's be old-fashioned carnival barkers. Let's run our rallies like game shows. Let's wear costumes and do skits as politicians taking payola from corporate lobbyists. We have nothing to lose, and it's a *plus*!"

I left Lisa writing notes at lightning speed, still buzzing with the thrill of our ideas. I remembered the line from a favorite Dylan song—*When you ain't got nothing, you got nothing to lose.* A campaign slogan written by one of the century's great-est social commentators? Bring on the bumper stickers.

And like that, as if the musical reference conjured her up from Boulder, I looked down the aisle to the volunteer sign-up table and saw Janine.

Brady bounded down the aisle and almost knocked me over. He lay on the floor, begging me to rub his belly. I obliged.

Janine approached me carefully, as if I were not the same guy she'd been going out with only six weeks before. She wore her plaid kilt with a striped top and sheepskin boots. I couldn't help grinning when I saw her.

"Hey, Mark." She extended her hand as if we were barely acquaintances. "I guess I should call you Larry now."

"Janine, I called you ten times before we went public, but you were still away. I am so sorry."

"No, *I'm* sorry. You tried to tell me how much you hated those shopping trips, and I wouldn't listen. You were right; it was such a waste of time." She gestured at the flurry of activity around us. "You obviously had much bigger plans."

Brady continued to roll around on the floor. "This was actually a spur-of-the-moment thing," I answered.

She let out one of her giant laughs. "No one runs for president on impulse."

I shrugged. "Why not? I do most everything else that way."

"Like leave? I should've known something was up with that dying grandmother story."

I tried to explain about being kidnapped and coming back east, but even to me the excuse sounded pathetic.

"It doesn't matter," she said. "We just flew out to congratulate you and see if I could help you back in Boulder."

"Absolutely. We're building a network of people out west. I'd love to have someone I trust there." I introduced her to Greg, our western states coordinator, then left for a meeting with Peter.

Beth caught up with me as I headed toward the stage.

"I haven't seen a get-up like that since your mom was the cafeteria monitor in junior high. She always wore the wackiest outfits, God bless her."

I nodded, knowing if I didn't dole out information, Beth would go crazy.

"Did she fly in from Colorado? I recognize her from when the investigator and I tracked you down."

"Then you know her name is Janine," I said. "Not 'she.'"

Beth did her usual routine, running to catch up to me then blocking my path. "Are she and Lassie here to volunteer?"

"Yes. I set her up with Greg. We'll be seeing a lot more of her."

I resisted the temptation to turn around and check out the expression on Beth's face as I walked away.

This could actually be interesting.

Even with Simon hanging around 24/7,[51] Beth assumed

---

[51]Okay, he wasn't just hanging around; he was doing a lot of great work.

she would continue to be the only woman I could possibly be interested in. For a brief moment, I even thought about asking Janine to stay in Boston just to see what kind of reaction I could eke from Beth over an extended period of time. I dispensed with the idea, however, as being unfair to everyone involved.

Peter paced the theater office, sloshing his cup of coffee each time he turned. He'd been holed up here with the graphics people for the past several days.

"Tell me what you think." He pulled me over to the back wall, which was filled with several glossy photos. One was a picture of my gravestone, with JOSH SWENSEN engraved in large letters. Underneath the photo, the caption read, A VOTE FOR JOSH IS A VOTE FOR LARRY. HE'S LESS DEAD THAN MOST OF THESE OTHER STIFFS.

I spit my coffee across the room.

"I'm kidding!" Peter said. "We're getting a little punchy after working twenty hours straight."

The guy was killing me.[52]

We brainstormed about other slogans and graphics for several hours before Janine came knocking on the door looking for me. I introduced her to Peter, who gave her a quick hug. Janine and I planted ourselves on the stairs leading to the stage.

Her hair was now black with streaks of purple. I asked her where she was staying. She pulled out the Lonely Planet guide to Boston from her pack. "There's a hostel near B.U. that takes dogs. I'll just grab the T."

---

[52]Pun intended.

I told her I wouldn't hear of it, that she and Brady could stay with Peter and me back at the house. She wove her arm through mine. "Maybe you'll come back to Boulder—to campaign, I mean."

I told her we'd be out there next month.

"Good," she said. "We'll have the best rally the town's ever seen."

"I'll make sure we don't schedule it on a Monday so you can introduce us." I leaned over and kissed her, unfazed by Beth now standing in front of me waving a piece of paper.

"You better see this, Josh." She handed me the paper, a printout from the Larry Web site. It was an entry dated just minutes before.

I didn't need to read the entire message to figure out who'd sent it.

Betagold.

WELL, JOSH. I HATE TO SAY "I TOLD YOU SO" BUT I WAS RIGHT ALL ALONG, WASN'T I? RIGHT ABOUT YOU NOT BEING DEAD, RIGHT ABOUT YOU LYING TO THE WORLD, BUT MOST OF ALL, RIGHT ABOUT YOU BEING A COWARD. ARE YOU HAPPY NOW? HAPPY TO BE BACK IN THE SPOTLIGHT, THE SPOTLIGHT I PUT ON YOU IN THE FIRST PLACE? WOULDN'T BE WHERE YOU ARE NOW IF IT WEREN'T FOR ME, ISN'T THAT SO? AND RUNNING FOR PRESIDENT? I THINK RUNNING IS THE OPERATIVE WORD HERE, JOSH, DON'T YOU? YOU SHOULD RUN— ALL THE WAY BACK TO WHERE YOU'VE BEEN HIDING. YOU DON'T THINK YOU HAVE A CHANCE OF FINISHING THIS CAMPAIGN, DO YOU? I USED TO GIVE YOU (A LITTLE) MORE CREDIT THAN THAT. SEE YOU SOON. YOUR PAL, BETAGOLD

"She's sick," Beth said. "I told Charlene to delete the message off the board."

"It was just a matter of time before she started up again," I said.

Janine shoved her hand toward Beth. "I'm Janine. Congratulations."

"On?"

Janine looked puzzled. "On running for vice president, on being the first teenage girl to have a voice in a national election."

"Oh, is that what I am now? Some kind of national voice?"

I pulled Beth aside. "Stop being such a bitch—don't you think we have bigger problems right now? She's on our side."

"She? I thought her name was Janine." Beth headed toward the kitchen without looking back.

Janine put on her fake fur jacket.[53] "I hope I didn't cause any—"

"No, it's nothing. She's just worried about betagold. Last time she saw her, it was an ugly scene." Visions of Tracy Hawthorne in my living room, Beth screaming, and whirring cameras flooded back to me.

"I know. I went to the library and did some research on your past life. You two have been through a lot together."

Janine looked so sweet and uncomplicated, I suddenly felt stupid for comparing her to Beth while we were going out. I gave her my key and address and told her I'd meet her back at the house later.

I took a long walk through town to shake off the stench of betagold.

---

[53]Which she'd sprayed with red paint in a sicko attempt at recreating a PETA protest. So funny.

What was her problem? Why couldn't some people let others voice their opinions without getting so bent out of shape? Why couldn't we agree to disagree? I didn't know what to do—set up a meeting with betagold and defuse the situation or just ignore her and continue to run an honest and respectful campaign. I had to fight the urge to bike over to Bloomingdale's and seek my mother's counsel. Instead, I met with our logistics and security teams. I couldn't obsess about betagold; there were too many other things that needed my attention.

• • •

Lisa had convinced me that we needed to bring in an outside media consultant to meet with us. I nixed his ideas for phone canvassing, polls, and direct mail in favor of old-fashioned rallies. I wanted to spread the word without bothering people. He called me naive and left in a huff.

Simon stroked his beard thoughtfully. "Personal appearances are great, but it's a damn big country."

I'd just spent the past two years traveling the back roads coast to coast. Did Simon think he was telling me something I didn't know?

"Look," I said. "It's the only way I'm going to do this—meet people, listen to them, look them in the eye. I mean, it's not like we're going to *win*. I just want to get people to vote."

I could tell by his face this disappointed Simon. He had garnered every activist accolade there was; he didn't like to lose.

ELECTION COUNTDOWN
FEBRUARY:
ON THE ROAD

The experience of traveling cross-country now was diametrically opposed to my last trip. First off, this one was voluntary. Secondly, I was surrounded by friends, and as much as I am someone who is happiest alone, I enjoyed having people around for a change.

Every consultant we had talked to said the real clout was in fund-raisers and photo ops. But rallies still seemed like the best way to get in close with people, the country's real natural resource.

We tried to make our rallies as original as possible. At one bowling alley in Baltimore, we staged an opera with Beth and me wearing Viking helmets and singing.[55] We did a whole game show spoof in Ohio giving answers to questions shouted out from the audience. All this gave our opponents more ammunition, of course. If we got any press at all, it was to vilify us. I was crucified for not taking the role of president seriously.

This criticism kept me staring at the ceiling into the wee hours; I didn't care what anyone said, I was not being cynical

---

[55]The MP3 file was Kazaa's number seventeen download in Baltimore that week.

88

Lisa couldn't wait to introduce me to an MIT freshman she'd found to run our Internet operations. His name was Tim, and he could code HTML and Java faster than most people could boot their computers.

"I'm warning you, though—he's Mr. Techspeak," Lisa whispered.

My second language. I followed Lisa to the computer room and shook Tim's hand.

He buzzed around the room with so much energy, it was as if he were the one plugged into the wall, not the computer.

"I grok the vibes here," he said.

"Yeah, but can you grep the system by the end of the week?" I asked.

When he told me no sweat, I welcomed him aboard.

Beth dragged me outside and said Peter wanted to see us. We exited the theater, but couldn't find him until a bright yellow school bus pulled up to the curb and opened its doors, revealing Peter in the driver's seat.

I couldn't stop laughing.

"Katherine found it on eBay for two thousand dollars," he said. "I had Billy drive me out to Andover to pick it up."

"So much of our platform is education," I said. "This is perfect."

High in the driver's seat, Peter looked like a five-year-old eating chocolate for the first time. "Katherine really wanted to help. She wishes you the best."

I nodded, still unsure of the people I'd grown up with playing new roles in my life. Had everyone else changed or was it me?

I went back in and called the volunteers over for a quick ride. They ran to the back of the bus as if they were still in junior high.[54] We hooted and hollered our way through town, the first real blowing-off-steam session of our fledgling campaign. I tried not to dwell on the political consultant's words. Was my head buried in the sand on this one? Was I wasting the time and energy of these chanting volunteers who filled the bus beside me?

It was a fine line to walk between being idealistic and practical; I hoped I was smart enough to balance the two this time.

---

[54]Not me; I always sat up front alone.

QUALITY OF LIFE

JUNK FOOD IS NOW A $110 BILLION INDUS
CHILDHOOD OBESITY AND DIABETES
RAMPANT. DO WE PUT HEALTHY FOODS
SCHOOLS OR BAN TV ADS? NO, WE APPR
STOMACH STAPLE OPERATIONS FOR K

THE AVERAGE U.S. CHILD WATCHES 1,500 HOURS OF TV A YEAR AND SPENDS 900 HOURS AT SCHOOL.

IN 1987 THE NUMBER OF U.S. SHOPPING CENTERS SURPASSED THE NUMBER HIGH SCHOOLS.

ALMOST 50 PERCENT OF U.S. HIGH SCHOOL GRADUATES ARE FUNCTIONALLY ILLITERATE.

THE NUMBER OF PEOPLE IN U.S. PRISONS AND JAILS TRIPLED BETWEEN 1980 AND 1996.

HAVE WE FOUND A CURE FOR CANCER, HEART DISEASE, OR AIDS? NO. BUT WE DID INVENT VIAGRA, LIPOSUCTION, AND BOTOX. WAY TO GO!

about the office of the president. On the contrary, I was so optimistic that things could be better in this country that I was willing to work around the clock to contribute to such a goal. Americans were generous and open and ambitious; I believed that in my bones. But how could you justify such goodness with the rising climate of inequality and fear?

In every part of the country, I began our sessions not by talking but by listening. I spent hours at each campaign stop hearing the stories of people who had lost their jobs or couldn't pay their bills. I listened to their ideas for solutions instead of spewing forth my own canned answers. Their suggestions fueled us with an urgency that kept our campaign vital.

On the bus, we listened to music and sang. The girls on the staff would howl with laughter at Simon's mangled lyrics.

"'She's got a chicken to ride'?" Susie, our travel coordinator, asked. "Talk about butchering a Beatles song. . . ."

At each rest area, Simon surrounded himself with a crowd of admirers while Beth and I edited speeches. But as each night rolled around and some people paired off, Simon and Beth continued to be together. Unfortunately, I was always odd man out.[56]

· · ·

In every town we hit, our first stop was usually a school. And what Beth brought to these rallies was invaluable. When she went into a classroom, it wasn't just to pose for pictures, reading

---

[56] You'd think there'd be *some* perk to being the guy running for president, yes?

books to a group of kindergarteners while the cameras clicked away. Instead she set up assemblies with seniors and registered them to vote. She ran mock debates in the middle schools, discussing such topics as gun legislation and human rights.[57]

Only I could tell the grip of exhaustion that began to take hold. After weeks of speeches, meetings, and little sleep, Beth started to snap at things that never before would've dented her consciousness. I kept trying to talk her into joining me for yoga, but she wouldn't. Simon tried to get her to slow down, bringing her miso soup between meetings, urging her to eat. She often responded with increasing annoyance and impatience. I almost felt bad for the guy, his love for her so obvious to anyone who saw them together.

Not that I intervened on his behalf; I let him suffer.

I wondered if some of her annoyance hinged on the fact that our next stop was Boulder. But as usual, my telepathic connection with Beth ended at trying to figure out how she felt about me.

The first thing I did when we got to Boulder was run up Mount Sanitas full-out. I'd missed the view and the crisp air slapping my lungs as the altitude changed. I stood on the ledge overlooking the town for almost an hour. I caught sight of a deer, which only made me feel worse about neglecting my animal studies. But the quick jaunt into nature temporarily quenched my desire to connect with the earth.

---

[57]The word *mock* doesn't do these kids justice; they were into it.

Janine had assembled almost seven hundred people for the rally at the university and another nine hundred at Red Rocks Amphitheatre. She wore pants with leather patches that looked like the inside of a Mustang convertible. Her hair was braided on the top of her head; tiny rubber monkeys adorned her earrings. Beth rolled her eyes when she saw her, but I thought Janine looked great.

"I know you didn't want to do the whole one-thousand-dollars-a-plate fund-raiser thing, so I thought of something better." Janine held up a poster. BAKED BEAN SUPPER WITH LARRY, PRESIDENTIAL CANDIDATE—THREE DOLLARS A PLATE.

Simon looked as if he'd collapse in laughter. "Well, that should cover our gas money for getting out here."

Janine looked him dead-on. She no longer seemed the same carefree girl from a few months before. "We've got almost twenty-five thousand people coming," she said. "Seventy-five thousand dollars."

"That's almost a third of the people in Boulder!" I was shocked at Janine's transformation.

"Lots of them are from Denver," Janine answered. "I was actually aiming for more, but I'm happy with this."

The logistics were staggering. How do you feed twenty-five thousand people, let alone meet some of them and get your message across? But Janine had every angle covered, taking advantage of local arenas and theaters. Using a staggered schedule, Beth and I would be able to have several rallies throughout the day. Even Beth had to admit Janine had organized something on a whole different scale than the other state organizers had.[58] The CD compilation Janine had put together had the young crowd stomping its feet before I took the stage.

Be Radical—Vote!

Watch TV.

Consume.

Don't make waves.

Work.

Die.

Is this the American Dream?

No, but it's the way most of us live our lives these days.

Notice that voting is not on this list. That's because only a minority of people vote in this country. The media love to use such words as landslide and trend when they describe elections, but when you break it down, it's only a small percentage of the population that decides the fate of our country.

Only 39 percent of all registered voters bothered to vote in the 2002 midterm elections; about half—17 percent—voted Republican. The media called the event a mandate of the people. Since when is 17 percent a mandate of anything? This small percentage of the American

---

[58]Whenever the media describe a large, successful fund-raiser, their yardstick is always how much money was raised, not how many people got to interact with the candidate or were moved to political action.

population decided who now controls our House and Senate.

You want to know government's dirty little secret? It's more outrageous than any other conspiracy in our history, more telling than the Pentagon Papers or Watergate.

POLITICIANS DON'T WANT YOU TO VOTE. Voting means you're passionate about the issues, enough to get out and do something about it. Voting challenges the status quo. But the politicians in Washington don't want you to do that. They want you to sit back and enjoy the ride while they drive our country down the path of Big-Business handouts, which in turn, increases their own campaign war chests. They love low voter turnout; it means the stalwarts will be the only ones out there carrying the party torches while the rest of us scratch our heads and wonder why our voices aren't being heard.

People think by not voting they're casting a vote against the system. WRONG! By not voting you're letting a small minority determine the policy for the rest of us. WE CAN'T SIT BACK ANYMORE! The most radical thing we can do is actually something as pedestrian as voting.

News flash—decisions are made by the people who show up!

If 90 percent of the people in this country actually cast their ballots on election day, the Administration would head for the hills! How about this for a crazy idea? Instead

of sitting at home on your couch watching reality TV, you
invest in your OWN reality and vote. I don't even care who
you vote for! Whatever we do, we have to stop the hijack-
ing of our government; it's OURS; let's take it back.

We don't need to bomb a country halfway around the
world in the name of democracy.

We can fight for it right here.

That's how important your ballot is in November.

Be a rebel, be a radical—vote!

The country needs YOUR input.

ARE YOU LETTING YOUR VOICE BE HEARD?

When I walked off the stage, the students were applaud-
ing in a slow, steady beat. I actually felt the energy shift in the
room. We were making a difference. That is, until Beth pulled
me into the hall.

"What's the matter?"

She sucked on a strand of her hair. "I'm not sure. I think
that was too much information."

"People need information to make an informed decision."

"Just because you're an information junkie doesn't mean
the rest of us are. Anyway, it seemed like you were losing a few
of them, that's all."

"What are you talking about?"

"The campaign is supposed to be geared toward kids who
are voting for the first time and you're spewing statistics and
percentages. Let's face it—those numbers are boring."

"What, you think most people are too focused on their own lives to care about any of this?"

"It's just that I was watching these kids up front. They were smiling; they were cheering. Then I saw you lose them. Saw the passion drain from their eyes right in front of me."

"Maybe it's me," I said. "Maybe I'm a bad speaker. I probably should have stayed in my basement, grinding out sermons anonymously."

"It's hard. How do you take what we care about and make it palatable for everyone?"

I tried to control the edginess in my voice. "It *isn't* palatable, most of it *sucks*. And no one will be motivated to change things unless they hear about it!"

She leaned against the wall again, this time sliding down till she was sitting on the floor. "It just sounds so dry. I don't know if there's any way around it."

Janine found us in the hall and jumped into my arms. "You were great. There are over four hundred kids registering to vote right now."

Beth smiled and bounded down the hall. "But then again I could be wrong."

• • •

Peter called to say he was now making three bank trips a week to deposit the rolls of pennies from the barrels we'd set up at the mom-and-pop stores across New England. We discussed our strategy for going nationwide with our fund-raising.

"We might even have enough to run a local ad or two," he said.

"Really? That would make up for the fact that most people in America still don't even know we're running." (Christina Aguilera's new video was getting more media attention than our presidential campaign.)

"Have you seen the Web site?" Peter asked. "Some kid came up with the idea of your supporters spending a dollar on a lottery ticket and sending it to campaign headquarters for you to scratch. If it's a winner, you keep the money for your campaign, no strings attached."

"I'm *against* lottery tickets," I said. "They're just another way to keep poor people hoping their luck will change. The government sells gambling instead of putting effective programs into place."

"Well this kid started a trend, and it's spreading like wildfire. I scratched thirty-nine tickets today."

I put my hands over my ears to block them. "Don't tell me! I don't want to know."

I had to care about money; we needed it to get our message out. All the fund-raisers we'd had and pennies we'd collected added up to more than thirty thousand dollars, which we'd stretched as far as we could. It was a far cry from the billion dollars the Democrats and Republicans had spent last election, but I still felt guilty about it.

That night back in Janine's apartment as I sat on the floor playing with Brady, waves of doubt kept me from sleeping.

Who was I to be hawking a better way? I did a great job of listing our government's faults, but could I do any better? One day of tough decision-making might send me racing for the Oval Exit. Was I in too deep this time, even for me? The tug-of-war I played with Brady couldn't compare to the one going on inside my head.

Over the next few weeks, my "opponents" turned up the volume on disparaging my candidacy. The president said I was wasting my time, as well as the time of the voters. One senator said he admired my environmental stand, but my lack of political experience made me woefully inadequate for the job. Another agreed that campaign finance reform was one of the biggest issues facing us today, but he thought my ideas on the subject were naive. One congresswoman even called me to brainstorm about grassroots fund-raising, then wished me luck.

We hooked up with rockthevote.org, which ran our touring schedule on their Web site. They were committed to increasing teen registration too and were happy to endorse our philosophy.

Lisa had scheduled spots with several call-in radio shows. We talked with listeners about corporate welfare and violence in the schools. Most of the people who called in were thoughtful and made good arguments for their positions.

The producer put through the final call.

"I know why you're doing this," the caller said.

I recognized the voice immediately.

"You just love being the center of attention, don't you?" betagold asked.

"Actually," I answered, "I'd much prefer to be left alone. I'm speaking out because I think the average person's concerns aren't being addressed."

Beth made a "cut" motion at her neck, telling the producer to stop the call. I shook my head; let betagold speak.

"You can't win," she said. "Even if you were thirty-five, you wouldn't get enough votes."

"Our current president didn't get enough votes either. Who knows?"

"Your views are un-American," she said. "We need to stand behind our government, not criticize it."

"Since when is exercising your right to free speech con- sidered un-American?" I asked. "It's so important, it's the first amendment they wrote. Can't get more apple pie than that."

"You have no idea what goes on in Washington," she said. "There are policies and decisions you know nothing about. Your opinions are superficial."

I wanted to tell her that in my doubting moments I agreed with her. "People always say that when kids throw in their two cents," I finally answered. "It's all about wanting us to keep our mouths shut."

Betagold's voice was barely a whisper. "You're only going to get hurt."

Beth rolled her chair toward the mike. "Are you threatening us?"

99

"There are worse things than violence," betagold answered. "You'll see."

The dial tone hummed into the studio.

When the producer went to commercial, Beth yanked off her headset. "This isn't funny," she said. "I don't trust her."

"Yeah, I'm real worried one senior citizen is going to derail our campaign."

"You're forgetting how long she tracked you down. Finding you was her full-time job. You shouldn't underestimate how much she wants to ruin this for you."

"She's not violent," I said. "She just wants to be heard."

"Well, I'm calling my cousin Tony and beefing up security. I want to go over every detail of our itinerary and make sure there are no loose ends."

"Susie and Tony have it covered," I said. "But knock yourself out."

Beth looked at me with so much feeling, I nearly burst. "I don't want anything to happen to you. I already lost you once. I can't lose you again."

"That's not going to happen." As I was just about to try my luck and kiss her, my cell rang.[59]

"Our entire system crashed," Peter shouted. "The Web site, the lists of volunteers, our travel schedule—all of it."

I asked him how that could have happened since I'd loaded the security software onto the system myself.

---

[59]Peter had insisted I get one for the campaign. I *hated* it—and not just because it rang at inopportune moments like this one.

"Somebody hacked on with some kind of virus. Tim was at the terminal when a red peace sign came up and just exploded like an atomic cloud with this demonic laugh. The guy's in a frenzy trying to figure out what happened. We might have to start from scratch."

I hung up and told Beth the news.

"It's not like betagold didn't warn us," she said.

"If she's behind it."

"Like anyone else cares enough to bother?"

• • •

When I called Janine in Boulder that night, she insisted on flying to Boston to help Tim re-enter the data.[60] I put her on speakerphone with Tim to assess the damage.

"This is information assassination," Janine said. "It'll cost us weeks."

"The system is completely fragged," Tim said. "I tried to kluge it the best I can, but it's gone."

"Wormhole?"

"Yup—I nearly dumped core when I found it."

I swallowed the familiar feeling of paranoia tinged with fear, then reminded myself I was running for office on a NON-fear platform.

I kept coming back to a favorite biology textbook. There was a section on rhizomes, plants that spread an elaborate,

---

[60]She was such a trouper, Tim made room in his office and dragged in a desk for her when she was in town.

interlocking root system underground.[61] Then suddenly—*wham!*—new plants sprout up all over the place, connected by roots you didn't even know were there. I thought about our headquarters back in Boston with dozens of people working so hard and hoped all this backbreaking effort would result in a strong, vital network that would spread and blossom sometime soon.

[61]Talk about a GRASSROOTS effort.

ELECTION COUNTDOWN

MARCH 2:

THE MASSACHUSETTS PRIMARY

We wound our way back to Boston, weary from more than a month on the road. The president had his party's nomination wrapped up, while the Democrats continued to duke it out in the primaries. Thankfully, because I was the only Peace Party candidate, we didn't have to implement a primary strategy.

We had just finished a rousing three-hour service in a Baptist church in Hartford when Peter called.

"Are you sitting down?" he asked.

"No, I'm pacing around outside like a madman. This gospel music rocks."

"Four point three million dollars," he said.

I sat on the curb. "What are you talking about?"

"A Powerball ticket a kid from Tucson sent in. You won."

I felt the schism begin inside me, between the need for campaign funds and my own anti-materialism. "I can't accept it," I said.

"It was a donation," Peter said. "No special interests to serve."

"I know, but still . . ."

"Paid out from the Lottery Commission. The state government will be paying you to compete against the feds. Don't you love the irony?"

Peter knew what he was doing; pitching the subversiveness of the situation definitely made the whole thing easier to digest.

"Okay," I said. "Let's kick around some ideas."

"Are you nuts?" Peter shouted. "What do you think I've been doing all these months? Check out your laptop; I'll download some clips. We can blitz Massachusetts for the rest of the week."

"I don't care about the primaries," I said.

"They're as important as the election. Trust me on this, okay?"

I hung up and called Beth and Simon to the back of the church.

"Oh my God. Oh my God," Beth said when I told her the news. "The campaign can finally get some attention."

"This changes everything," Simon said. "We can afford polls and—"

"No polls. I just want people to hear where we stand on the issues, not see where I rank in some rigged popularity contest."

The video clip filled the screen of my laptop. Republicans shaking hands with oil company executives cashing in lucrative Iraqi contracts. Democrats and CEOs making deals on a golf course. Lobbyists racing from office to congressional office. The montage of these heavy-hitters was crosscut with images of overcrowded classrooms, cleaning ladies, factory workers, poverty-stricken children. The whole commercial was set to the song "Money."

"I love it," Simon said. "As long as we don't have to pay Pink Floyd for the rights."

I scrolled through Peter's e-mail. "It says here they donated them."

"Good job on Peter's part," Beth said.

"Looks like Janine negotiated it."

It was almost fun to watch Beth struggle to keep the smile on her face.

Simon asked when we could run the ad.

"Peter wants to line one up for tonight. Then five times a day all week."

Simon packed up his things. "We can visit a lot of cities between now and Tuesday."

Beth still wasn't sold. "We've got nothing to win in the primary."

"More like nothing to lose," I said.[62]

"Four point three million dollars." Beth whistled. "Do you know how many people that could feed? Or cover with health insurance?"

"Spreading the news about government inadequacy is part of the solution too," I said. "Let's go."

• • •

---

[62]When in doubt, quote Dylan.

When we saw the commercial during the local news that night in Northampton, we screamed so loudly I expected the motel owner to come pounding on the door. The next day we hit the road even earlier than usual, visiting schools, hospitals, grocery stores, and pizza parlors. We still weren't getting any press, but we met a lot of great people.

The night of the primaries, we stopped by as many voting spots as physically possible in one day. From Somerville to Billerica to Leominster to Hingham, we shook hands and answered questions while hundreds of our supporters stood in the cold winter air holding signs.

It was almost ten at night by the time we left for headquarters. Simon had one of those battery-operated TVs tuned in to the returns.

"Shhhh!" he yelled as the lead story kicked in.

The airbrushed newsman gushed about the state's voter turnout, the highest in seventy-five years.

"Forty-three percent!" Simon shouted.

As if the news anchor had heard us, he continued. "Equally amazing is the turnout of voters aged eighteen to twenty-four. A whopping 54 percent."

"That's almost twice as many young people voting as the last presidential election!" Beth said. "And primaries are always much less."

"Tallies are still coming in, but—hold on to your hats, folks—underage local candidate 'Larry' Swensen has walked away with 12 percent of the vote! It's not his primary, but a nice percentage of voters wrote him in anyway!"

Someone might as well have thrown a match into the gas tank, because the bus exploded.[63]

"You're news now," Simon said.

"This is incredible," Beth screamed.

The image of the rhizome flashed into my head. The fruits of our labor might actually be taking hold.

"It's too bad it took so much money to get us this far," I said.

Simon barely contained his disdain. "Of course it takes money—is that just dawning on you now?"

Beth tried to ease the tension. "It'll cost *some* money, but not nearly as much as the other candidates are spending."

I nodded, knowing she was right.

The clamor in the bus was so deafening, I barely heard my cell ring. I waved my hands to quiet everyone. "Peter? You did it!" I shouted.

"Not only that," Peter said. "We got the ten thousand signatures and the twelve non-party electors like any other candidate."

"I still can't run because of my age."

"No, but you can be a write-in. There's enough momentum."

He told me he had another call and he'd get right back to me. Beth jumped into my lap. "We're at the grown-ups' table now!"

"Are you up for this?" I asked.

---

[63] I didn't really appreciate his use of the phrase "walked away with," as if I'd waltzed in without doing any work. We'd been working tirelessly for months, but I wasn't about to quibble with such amazing results.

"Hell, yes. Let's work it for all it's worth."

The phone rang again. "Peter," I said. "I still can't believe it."

"This isn't Peter," the voice answered.

My instinct was to throw the phone out the window at the sound of betagold's voice. "How'd you get this number?"

"Don't celebrate too much," she said. "The bottom's falling out soon."

"This doesn't have anything to do with you," I responded. "And how did you get this number?"

"I know more than you think I do, Larry. I suggest you savor this victory, because it's your last."

As soon as I slammed the phone shut, it rang again.

"Even bigger news," Peter said. "People are signing up to be Peace Party candidates all across the country. Hundreds of eighteen-year-olds are running for senate and representative seats in their home states. It's a movement!"

The news was shocking. After all this hard work, we actually were making a difference. People everywhere were picking up the gauntlet.

But it was hard not to think about betagold.

I told Peter to cancel my cell and get me a new number no one else had access to. I told him to change all the passwords on our software and check with Tony in security.

Beth pulled me aside after I hung up. "That was betagold before, wasn't it?"

"Forget it. We should be happy."

"She's inside, Josh, I swear. And everyone's been through top-level clearance."

I told Beth we'd have a meeting back in Boston with all the directors, try to get a handle on where betagold was getting her information. I slung my arm over her shoulder. "Can we just enjoy this moment?"

"No, you're right. You should really be proud."

"We." I kissed her, not caring that Simon was standing in the aisle beside us.

He ushered Beth away. "We're here. Let's go."

I hadn't even noticed we were back at headquarters. I sucked up all my nervous energy and readied myself for the reporters' questions.

Simon turned to me as I gathered my things. "I suggest you savor that kiss, because it was your last."

He was soon swallowed into the pack of reporters and photographers stationed outside our headquarters.

What worried me more than the interviews, more than being an official write-in candidate for the president of the United States, was how much Simon had just sounded like betagold.

PART THREE

"A patriot must always be ready to defend
his country against his government."

Edward Abbey

ELECTION COUNTDOWN
APRIL:
FINALIZING A PLATFORM

Along with the daffodils and crocuses, the campaign began to bloom.

Our impressive showing in the Massachusetts primary was followed by surprising primary results in Maryland, Louisiana, and Wisconsin. It seemed the campaign was gaining momentum solely by challenging the status quo.

The most important item on our agenda was coming up with a cohesive platform. We'd been raising important issues for almost four months, but now we needed to offer real solutions. Education, diversity, human rights, the environment, crime, the economy . . . I was up to my eyeballs in sticky notes.

Beth looked over my shoulder as I compiled a first draft.

"I don't see anything here about women's rights," Beth said. "We still earn seventy-five cents for every dollar a man earns."[64]

I handed her my pen and told her to go for it. She wrote for several minutes, then stopped.

---

[64]African-American women, sixty-five cents; Latinas, fifty-eight. Scary, huh?

"It's much easier coming up with everything that's *wrong* with the system," she said. "Putting together effective programs is more difficult."

"That's why it's a work in progress." I tucked my notebook into my pack, knowing I'd be up all night obsessing.

"I just left Tony," Beth said. "He and I hired that investigator I used in Denver to run security clearance checks on the entire staff. Lisa, Tim, Susie, Janine. Everybody checks out."

"Simon too?"

"Simon, Peter—everyone but you."

"Very funny. I'll say it again—you're in the wrong business."

"I'm just trying to protect us," Beth said. "We can't afford another episode like last time."

The campaign still hadn't recovered from the computer virus, but Tim had cobbled together a new database system that was finally up and running. We kept our fingers crossed.

• • •

Bloggers were another alternative news source Beth and I constantly reviewed for feedback. These people posted their opinions and thoughts on their Web logs, thereby increasing the amount of exposure and discourse on the issues we raised. Most politicians decried the bloggers as "amateur journalists," but Beth and I found many of the sites informative and refreshing.

The blogger sites I returned to often were the ones with views opposite my own. My thoughts about the state of the country were opinions, obviously, and I enjoyed debating other passionate citizens point for point on the best solutions. Beth usually had to drag me away from the computer kicking and screaming.

"What's this person ranting about now?" she asked. "What picture in the *Post*?" I immediately went to the *Denver Post* Web site.

I had expected to take several hits because of my inexperience and age, but I didn't expect to see a photo of me from my Boulder days wearing a POLO sweater on the front page of a major newspaper. The accompanying exposé slammed me for not living up to my anti-materialistic beliefs. Letters on the op-ed pages of several other papers decried my hypocrisy about consumerism and workers' rights. My own Web site logged thousands of angry responses from betrayed supporters.

When we told Peter, he kicked into spin-control mode and set up several interviews. I answered every reporter's question as honestly as possible. Yes, the photos were actually of me. Yes, there was a period of several months last year when my strict philosophy and discipline had slipped. No, I didn't feel like a hypocrite running on an anti-consumerism platform; everyone makes mistakes. Yes, I'd been back to seventy-five possessions since January. The media milked the story to death.

"They say any publicity is good publicity," Simon offered.

"Well, they're wrong," I replied.

Janine took it hard.

"This is all my fault," she stammered. "If I hadn't dragged you shopping with me—"

"All the crimes against democracy people commit every day, and the press wants to hang me for buying some clothes with logos? Come on."

"I have no idea how they got that photo, I swear," Janine said.

I didn't tell her that Beth and I had spent quite a bit of time trying to figure out that very question. The photo had been taken at Chautauqua, where Janine and I had gone several times. I was standing next to a scenic overlook; anyone could've found me in the background of a photo and sent it in to the paper. But Beth was doubtful; even with Janine's security clearance, Beth thought she had to be involved. She called Greg, the western coordinator, and told him to keep his eyes open.[65]

The mudslinging didn't stop there.

Tabloids ran photos of me with Beth, me with Janine, me with every female volunteer they could find, trying to portray me as a political playboy—which would almost be flattering if it weren't such a joke.[66] They said any guy my age would have other things on his mind besides politics. The whole discussion was so tawdry I had to poke myself in the leg with my pen to stay awake during the reporters' questions.

---

[65] I went even farther but for a different reason—to prove Janine's innocence. I had Lisa call the *Post* to see who'd taken the photo. They said they'd received it anonymously.

[66] I could almost hear every girl I went to high school with howling at these allegations.

. . .

I took our fledgling platform for a test drive at Lexington High School. Because my suggestions for a better country had zero chance of being implemented, I decided to have some fun.

Peace Party Ideas for a Better Planet
- *SUVs are now considered buses; people driving them must pull over to bus stops and give others a ride.*
- *All assault weapons are hereby banned; the waiting period for a handgun is now a lifetime.*
- *Standardized testing, including SATs, will no longer be used in schools. Instead, students will be graded on critical thinking and innovative ideas.*
- *The tax on junk food will be 100 percent, with the proceeds funding universal health care.*
- *If the company you work for doesn't pay you enough to live, it must supply you with free housing to make up for it.*

The audience's expressions were priceless.[67] The reporters from the *Globe* and *Herald* raced out the door.

When I finished, Simon and Beth pounced.

"We were supposed to agree on the platform, remember?" Beth said.

---

[67]One administrator looked so angry, I swear she was about to rush the stage. I haven't made a teacher that mad since I Cling Wrapped the toilet seats in the teachers' lounge back in junior high.

"How do you expect to be taken seriously?" Simon added. "We look like amateurs."

"Good! There are too many lawyers and lobbyists involved in the process. We need a more homespun approach," I answered.

"This isn't *The Beverly Hillbillies,*" Beth said. "Our ideas have to hold up."

"To say nothing of messing with personal freedom," Simon said. "People *can* eat crap if they want to. Not everyone chooses to live their lives the way you do."

"I know that. But I'm trying to set us apart from the other candidates."

"Mission accomplished," Beth said.

"Admit it," I continued. "Every one of those suggestions would make this country a better place."

"According to you," Simon added.

A group of students waited by the bleachers. A kid with braces and a NO LOGO T-shirt gave me a high five.

"I've got one," he said. "No new golf courses. Instead, developers have to use the land for affordable housing."

"How about this?" a girl added. "Every tabloid and celebrity magazine has to be sold in a brown-paper wrapper so we don't get assaulted by JLo or Ashton Kutcher every time we leave the house."

I grabbed my book and jotted down notes. Simon shook his head and left for the bus. Beth stared at the scene in disbelief.

We thanked all the students for their thoughts and headed to the parking lot.

"Stop gloating," Beth said.

"Isn't this why you went to the trouble of bringing me back?" I teased. "For my ideas?"

She hip-checked me into a Jeep. "We'll get our butts kicked in the press tomorrow."

"Oh, come on." I pulled her behind a row of cars, out of Simon's view. "We're running a campaign that's honest, respectful, and original. Isn't that enough?"

She thought about it for a moment. "Every family with a three-car garage has to let a homeless family live there for free."

"Now you're talking."

She pulled me close, kissed me, then spun toward the bus.

I called after her. "Any girl going out with a British subject has to ditch him for the guy she grew up with."

She didn't turn around, but I could tell she was laughing. "Any guy who pretended he was dead and still has a girlfriend back in Colorado should keep his big, fat mouth shut."

I caught up and tackled her as she climbed the bus stairs. She slid into the seat with Simon anyway.

I don't care what other items stay on the platform, but this one's a definite: Any guy doing something as monumental as running for president shouldn't end up alone listening to a bus driver intern babble about a Red Sox losing streak while the girl he loves is sitting three seats back with someone else.

All the other programs can go, but *that* one's a keeper.

THE INCREASING GAP BETWEEN RICH AND POOR

SAMUEL JOHNSON SAID THAT "A DECENT PROVISION FOR THE POOR IS THE TRUE TEST OF CIVILIZATION." HOW DO WE RATE?

3 PERCENT OF THE POPULATION OWN MORE THAN 95 PERCENT OF PRIVATELY HELD U.S. LAND.

40 PERCENT OF THE AMERICAN WORKFORCE EARN WAGES BELOW THE FEDERAL POVERTY LEVEL. 40 PERCENT!

CORPORATE TAX SHELTERS COST THE AVERAGE AMERICAN OVER $10 BILLION A YEAR.

I DON'T GET IT—IF THE GOVERNMENT SETS THE POVERTY LEVEL AT $8.50/HOUR, WHY IS THE MINIMUM WAGE $5.15/HOUR?

ENRON HAD 881 OFFSHORE SUBSIDIARIES PAYING NO TAXES—WHY DON'T WE CLOSE THOSE LOOPHOLES?

IN 1965, CEOS MADE 44 TIMES MORE THAN THE AVERAGE BLUE-COLLAR WORKER; IN 2000, CEOS MADE 531 TIMES MORE.

40 PERCENT OF U.S. HOMELESS MEN ARE VETERANS, 20 PERCENT OF THE HOMELESS ARE EMPLOYED, AND 20 PERCENT ARE CHILDREN.

ELECTION COUNTDOWN
MAY:

LARRYFEST2

It was Bono's interest in my message that had first catapulted me into the stratosphere. This time around, it wasn't one person who jumpstarted the campaign; hundreds of people were intrigued by our non-traditional platform and contributed to the cause.

Matt Groening and his staff wrote Beth and me into a *Simpsons* episode seen by millions.[68] Jon Stewart and I had a spirited conversation on *The Daily Show*. Historian Howard Zinn met us at several locations and spoke to the crowds about third-party candidates throughout history.

That's not to say Bono wasn't crucial to our campaign. When he suggested Larryfest2, I jumped at the chance.

Normally a project that size would take several months or years to plan, but with our posse of volunteers and Bono's clout, we set it up in the same field in Maine, this time Memorial Day weekend instead of Fourth of July.

Janine was in heaven. She lined up the perfect mix of artists, running the spectrum from alternative to mainstream.

---

[68]She and I were at a dude ranch with Bart and Lisa. Hilarious.

And it wasn't only the acts she brought her creativity to; her ideas for the campsites and food stalls were equally inventive. In the spirit of the original Larryfest, we would charge no admission but would take donations and set up voter registration booths throughout the site. Even Bono suggested we charge *something*—it was a fund-raiser, after all—but the spirit of Larryfest was a force I didn't want to mess with, even for a cause as important as effecting social change.

There were a few other differences. This time around, Beth knew I was Larry.

Of course the rest of the world did too.

Whereas last time I had walked through the crowds anonymously, I now stopped to shake hands often and talk with the people who'd traveled to Maine to join in the festivities. As much as I wanted to make contact with the citizenry, I felt let down that I couldn't re-create the awe and camaraderie Beth and I had shared before. When the fireworks went off at midnight, all I could think about was the missed opportunity to consummate our relationship the last time.

As medallions of purple and green filled the sky, I heard a voice behind me.

"Remember that night?"

"What do you think I'm sitting here thinking about?"

Beth sat down beside me. "I wanted you so much."

"You did?" God, could I buy a clue?

"I was so mad you didn't make a move."

"Yeah, since *you're* so shy."

She asked if I was nervous about tomorrow. I told her that Simon, Janine, and Susie had it under control.

"I'm asking because Bono's not here yet. Neither is Dashboard Confessional or No Doubt."

I shrugged. "Maybe they're flying in early tomorrow. Did you ask Simon?"

"I would, but we're not speaking."

Now, *this* was interesting. "Is it because of . . ." I motioned to the space between us.

"God, Josh, everything is not about you, okay?"

"Yeah, I'm sure he wants to run through tomorrow's schedule when he's wondering if his girlfriend is going to cheat on him or not."

She looked at me as if I'd said something as grotesque as a racial slur. "I can't believe I came out here to remember that night with you and you're acting like such a jerk." She stood up and hurried back to her tent. When I called out to her, she didn't turn around, just flipped me the bird over her head.

Hopefully, no paparazzi were huddled in a nearby tent looking for exclusives.

. . .

The next morning's sunrise trumpeted a crystal-clear day. A perfect day to hang outside and listen to music.

If anyone were there to play it.

Janine pulled me away from a group of kids discussing their activist programs back in Nevada.

"You're not going to believe this," she said. "No one's here."

I pointed to the crowd of 400,000 just waking up.

"John Mayer, Foo Fighters, The White Stripes—none of them are coming."

"What?"

"I talked to Sheryl Crow this morning. They all got faxes from campaign headquarters saying the festival was canceled."

"From *our* campaign headquarters?"

"That's what I'm trying to tell you!" She handed me a piece of paper. "I had her fax me what she received. She was bummed. She really wanted to play."

Sure enough, the note was from our office, printed on official letterhead. And signed by me.

"Who—"

"The fax went out yesterday morning. There were tons of people going in and out of the office. It could have been anyone."

"What did Simon say?"

"I can't believe how well he's taking it. I'm a wreck. What are we going to do?" She moved nervously back and forth, like a four-year-old who had to use the bathroom.

"Who *is* here?"

"A few people who came in early—Norah Jones and Sting. I called Bono. He's leaving now."

"Why don't we start at nine as scheduled, see if they'll do longer sets?"

"That'll buy us an hour or two—then what? We don't want a Woodstock '99 on our hands."

I looked around at the peaceful crowd. "I doubt we're going to have looting and rioting here." Still, the thought of an atmosphere of chaos ratcheted up my fear twentyfold.

Simon ran over waving his clipboard. "It's a total and complete snafu."

I pulled my shirt over my head. "I refuse to believe that— refuse!"

Janine kicked into gear. "How about New York artists? Can't we fly people in?"

"Yeah, like we have Air Force One at our disposal," Simon answered.

"I'm trying to make the best of a bad situation here," Janine said. "Avril Lavigne played in Nashua last night. That's just a few hours away."

I stopped pacing. "Call Stacy in Manchester. Tell her to stand by."

Simon began punching numbers into his cell. "That's a start, but this crowd is expecting more than just a few acts."

Janine looked up from her laptop. "Coldplay is in Worcester, Badly Drawn Boy's in Portland—all we can do is ask, then make a relay with volunteers driving them up here."

"We can get drivers from the Web site too," Simon said. "Let's go."

Before Janine left to make her calls, I lifted her a foot off the ground and thanked her.

"Nobody's here yet. Let's see what we can do." As she ran to the tent, she yelled back over her shoulder. "Stall!"

What?

"Go up there," she said. "Do something!"

Was she serious?

But an hour later, the crowd was getting antsy. When I spotted some guy knocking over trash cans, I bit back the fear and headed to the stage.

"Thanks for coming out today," I said into the mike. "There have been lots of changes to the schedule—you'll have to work with us on this one. But hey, we're all about being spontaneous, right?"

No reaction at all. Me trying to act cool? Big mistake.

I decided to get right to it.

Bill of "Yeah, Rights"

Forget about the Bill of Rights!

(A collective gasp from the crowd.)

We the People have been sold a Bill of Goods!

The government and the media have been trying to scare the crap out of us for years, and guess what? It's working! We check the color-coded alert system and duct-tape our windows, assuming an atmosphere of fear and violence is the de facto state of the world. It doesn't make any sense.

And I swear, if I have to listen to another politician say our country's greatest natural resource is our children, I'm going to PUKE. "Leave no child behind"? Has anyone taken that lame political jingle and compared it to the statistics on education, child poverty, and gun violence? Hel-lo?

If you listen to politicians' words, kids are important; if you pay attention to their ACTIONS, we're not. Why can't they just admit the only resource they're concerned with is the amount of money our corporations rake in or our never-ending quest for world domination? I wish they'd just SAY it so we can finally stop hoping they're going to DO something about it.

Better yet—what are you doing about it? Are you going to peace marches? Calling your congressperson and senators? Are you working for campaign finance reform so we can stop this nonsense from the ground up?

You want things to be different—you make them different.

You want things to be better—you make them better.

I certainly don't have all the answers, but here are some things I'd do if I could get elected:

- Not one soldier goes to war unless every senator and congressperson sends a family member to the front lines first.
- For every sky-is-falling, world-is-going-to-end story on the news, the next story must be life-affirming and positive. Real balanced reporting.
- For every dollar spent on punishing criminals, another dollar will be spent on preventing crime with youth programs, education, and training.

There's plenty more where these came from. Stop by one of the many Peace Party tables to get more information. Vote for me, vote for somebody else, but just vote! And enjoy the concert!

The applause was explosive, thunderous. People were responding to my message in a big way. Maybe I *did* have something to offer this country after all.

Being bathed in the crowd's roar was one of the greatest moments of my life.

Until I realized the adulation was directed at Bono, who was walking toward me from across the stage. He shook my hand and hugged me; I waved to the not-paying-attention-to-me-at-all crowd and hurried off.

Bono started out by discussing the organization he'd founded called DATA.[69] Then he motioned for Norah Jones to join him, Sting too. As the performers trickled in, they sat in with this hodgepodge of a band. Aerosmith hopped on the Boston/Portland shuttle and were there by noon. Moby set up a techno booth where kids got to use synthesizers and cut demo tapes. Eve ran a hip-hop karaoke station that was mobbed all day. Chris Rock flew in from New York to host. By the end of the day, the band on stage consisted of the most eclectic, imaginative group of musicians ever assembled in one place. And the best part? Watching Janine backstage with

---

[69]Debt, AIDS, Trade in Africa.

a look of sheer joy. There wasn't another person loving the music more than she was.

As if it were possible to top that, Bono led the crowd in a chant of "202-456-1414!"—the phone number of the White House. He urged everyone at the festival to call and make their feelings known on everything from world debt to war. The all-star band wrapped up the night with a version of Neil Young's "Keep on Rocking in the Free World" that blew the roof off the place.[70] The crowd was a sea of signs—LARRY/BETH, peace symbols, and doves with branches. A day of music and sun transformed itself into a raucous peace rally,[71] which Janine caught on video.

In the end, Larryfest2 was a giant success.

When I found Beth slumped against one of the makeshift rooms backstage, she looked fried.

"We have to talk about what happened today," she said. "It could've been a disaster. We were lucky."

"The question is, who sent the fax?"

Beth looked as if she were about to cry. "It wouldn't be hard for either the Democrats or the Republicans to infiltrate our operation. Hell, a little bribe money would go a long way around here. Most of our staff is broke."

"You're not giving our volunteers and interns enough credit. They're all working their butts off just because they believe in our cause. I can't believe you're being so cynical."

---

[70]Okay, it was outdoors, but still . . .

[71]That's an oxymoron, I know, but it's true.

"I don't want to be," Beth said. "But we have to admit someone is out to get us."

It was hard not to think about another memory in this field last Larryfest. Waiting in line, toothbrush in hand, having a conversation with a friendly grandmother-type who would eventually destroy my life as I knew it. I scanned the crowd. Was betagold here again? Watching me at this very moment? Had she snuck into our headquarters early one morning and sent those faxes? Did she have people to help her—maybe a team? Were our opponents more threatened by our campaign than we thought? How far would members of the Establishment go to keep their giant slice of the Gross National Pie?

But as I looked across the field to the people pulling up tents and heading back to their homes across the country, I felt one thing—gratitude. We'd created something important, something real. When a young guy with a giant backpack spotted me and flashed a peace sign, I realized I was getting back more from the campaign than I was giving.

That thought almost offset the fact that we were being sabotaged, big time.

ELECTION COUNTDOWN
JUNE:
ON THE ROAD—AGAIN

Our tour bus looked more like it belonged to a rock band than a presidential campaign. CDs, soda cans, comic books, makeup, and videogames littered the aisles. The mess—and how many possessions they represented—drove me out of my mind. After lots of nagging and impassioned pleas, I finally gave up.[72] Beth didn't seem to notice.

What she did notice, however, was Simon's increasing popularity with the media. We all were happy with receiving mainstream coverage, but articles comparing Simon to Hugh Grant or describing Lisa as a "luscious lipstick lesbian" were not the kind of attention the campaign needed.

I looked out the bus window just in time to see a skein of Canada geese migrating in echelon formation. Traveling such distances is an enormous physical strain on the birds, but flying in a V lets them take advantage of the air from the bird in front of them. No such luck for the lead bird who has to wait for another in the flock to fly up and relieve him. Unfortunately, there was no such respite for me. The responsibility of

---

[72] Commander in chief? Not with this crowd.

guiding the rest of us to our destination sometimes seemed overwhelming and impossible.

Janine had joined us on the Albuquerque-to-Cheyenne leg, bringing along her videocamera to document our campaign. She ran down the aisle of the bus and collapsed into laughter next to me.

"Simon's the best!" she said. "He's singing 'wasted away again in my gorilla suit' at the top of his lungs."

"Everyone on the planet knows it's Margaritaville," I said. "I think it's all a giant put-on."

"Oh, come on."

Good old Janine, giving everyone the benefit of the doubt.

"He's flying back to Boston after today's speech," she said. "We're riding to the airport together."

"I thought you were staying?"

"Brady's acting up at the kennel. I've got to get back."

"And Simon?"

Janine explained that he had to check in with his professor at Harvard.

I had been counting the days till Janine arrived, but now Beth was the one who would be around. Conflicting thoughts ricocheted through my head like hormonal pinballs. Beth/Janine? Janine/Beth? I told myself I was being ridiculous. I was running for president; I had more important things to think about. Of course that didn't stop me from fixating on the relationship dilemma all day.

When we stopped at a sandwich shop in Santa Fe before the rally, I was shocked at how many supporters arrived carrying LARRY/BETH signs and wearing Peace Party buttons. Same thing at the auditorium. Then it dawned on me.

"Flash mobs," I told Beth. "They're all on their cell phones."

Sure enough, hundreds of kids were using their phones' text capabilities to send each other messages on our whereabouts.

Simon reached the same conclusion. "People wonder how Prince Harry goes to buy a pair of shoes and there are suddenly a hundred screaming teenage girls at the store within minutes. Texting."

"So this is good, right?" Beth asked.

"If you don't mind the whole celebrity business."[73] I took the stage.

Top Ten Reasons to Vote for Me for President

1. *Every workplace will have mandated recess. How can anyone be expected to make good decisions if you don't spend any time outdoors?*

2. *Lobbyists will be outlawed. Corporations will be given tax credits equal to the amount of time and effort spent on mentoring.*

3. *No candidate can spend more than ten million dollars to get elected—no loopholes, no exceptions. Every candidate will be given the same access to television advertising free of charge.*

---

[73]Not that a hundred screaming teenage girls was a *bad* thing. Did I just say that?

4. *World opinion does matter. I vow to work with the governments of other countries for solutions that make sense for all of us.*

5. *If kids under eighteen can't vote, why do they have to pay taxes? From now on, people who don't get to vote don't have to pay.*

6. *Last time I checked, the airwaves belonged to the people, right? The government will no longer under-write hatemongers who stir up negativity on their radio talk shows.*

7. *Ten percent of the defense budget will be spent on projects for peace.*

8. *To eliminate loopholes in the tax laws, all citizens pay a flat tax of 17 percent. Tax refunds are given only for time spent in community service.*

9. *Any country with human rights violations cannot do business with any U.S. corporation. No exceptions.*

10. *Since they're getting free advertising, clothing com-panies with logos must pay people to wear their clothes.*

My speech was followed by a terrific roar.[74] Afterward, I shook hands with hundreds of students at the voter registration table. A group of Radical Cheerleaders kept up the momentum.

"It's time to clean house," a young woman told me. "We need to get back to basics."

---

[74] And this time Bono was nowhere to be found.

"Don't let them shut you up," a guy my age shouted. "Keep up the good work!"

I talked to several more people before hiding behind some placards to catch Simon and Beth's goodbye. I was happy to see there was much less groping than there'd been six months ago when I first saw them together.

When I turned around, Janine was watching me watching them. The sadness in her eyes pinched me with guilt.

"Call me," she said. "Let me know how it goes in Wyoming."

"You've been amazing," I said. "I wish you could stay."

"Yeah, I'll bet." She hugged me goodbye and climbed into the volunteer's car with Simon.

I was loading the bus when someone came up behind me and covered my eyes. "Guess who?"

There was only one person who insisted on playing so many guessing games with me. "Peter?"

"Surprise!" He held up his garment bag. "Billy picked me up during your speech. I got sick of being at headquarters, wanted to hit the road for a few days and catch up on some work with you."

Was this a cosmic practical joke? Beth was finally free for the night and Peter was here to work?

Peter dropped his bag when he saw the inside of the bus. "Josh, this isn't professional!"

I told him I'd given up trying to organize the troops. He took over, handing out trash bags and paper towels. Maybe he should be our candidate.

• • •

At seven o'clock the next morning, Peter sat on the edge of my bed, shaking me awake.

"It's a good thing you're already lying down."

I buried myself deeper into my pillow. "What is it—another lottery ticket?"

"That was peanuts compared to this. You ready?"

I sat up on my elbows, as ready as a person who's slept only four hours a night for three months can be.

"Because of the bloggers and the flash mobs, yesterday's speech is everywhere."

"Good."

"People all across the country are demanding change, demanding answers," he said.

"It's about time."

"They're also demanding a twenty-eighth amendment."

"To lower the voting age to sixteen? People have been working on that for years."

"No. To change the minimum age that a person can run for president from thirty-five to eighteen."

"Get OUT of here!" I catapulted myself from the bed, suddenly charged with the pressure of 202 million eligible voters.

"Not because of me?"

"Of COURSE because of you! What do you think?"

"It'll never get through the House. It's not in their interest to pass it."

"Every senator and congressperson's phone is ringing off the hook. Their teenage constituents are demanding it."

I climbed back into bed. "This will blow over by tomorrow."

"Kids are involved, kids are voting. The people in Washington finally have to answer to them."

"It needs to be ratified by two-thirds of the Senate and House, then three-quarters of the state legislatures,"[75] I said.

"That'll never happen by November," Peter responded.

"Never in a million years," I agreed.

Still, the gravity of the situation hit me like a truckload of cement. Not only was someone proposing an amendment to the Constitution, they were doing it because of *us*. But more important—much more—if the amendment passed in a reasonable amount of time, I could legally run. And if I could *run,* it was statistically possible that I could *win.*

I ran to the bathroom, missed the toilet, and threw up all over the tiled floor.

I thankfully cleaned up the mess before Beth walked in.

"How'd you manage without Simon last night?" I asked.

"Josh, don't be a dope."

But when Peter told her about the amendment, Beth went from wisecracking to catatonic within seconds. "Oh my God, oh my God." She looked me in the eyes. "Is it wrong if I tell you I don't want it to pass?"

---

[75]See? I was paying attention in history class even though I was making a paint-by-number chess game at my desk.

"No, it's not wrong. It's honest." I turned away from her gaze. (Not because I had just thrown up all over myself, but because of what I was going to say next.)

"Should we withdraw?"

"We've got so many people depending on us," Beth said. "But forget it. The amendment will never happen."

"It'll die a quiet death. It was a nice gesture, though."

I washed up, then sat on the bed while Peter brewed coffee in the tiny pot on the desk. Beth stood in front of the television, transfixed by the image on the screen. The we-interrupt-your-regularly-scheduled-program clip showed thousands of teen-agers at the Capitol waving signs and banners.

WE WANT A SAY IN THINGS.

VOTE FOR AMENDMENT 28 OR YOU WON'T GET MY VOTE NEXT ELECTION.

WE WANT OUR GOVERNMENT BACK!

"This is more than a flash mob," I said.

"Nothing flashy about them," Peter added. "They're orga-nized and articulate."

I was screwed.

THE ENVIRONMENT

IT REQUIRES 2,640 GALLONS OF WATER TO PRODUCE ONE POUND OF EDIBLE BEEF.

57 PERCENT OF AMERICANS DON'T WANT DRILLING IN THE ARCTIC NATIONAL WILDLIFE REFUGE—WHY CAN'T CONGRESS FOCUS ON RENEWABLE ENERGY SOURCES INSTEAD?

5 PERCENT OF THE WORLD'S POPULATION LIVES IN THE U.S., BUT WE PRODUCE 50 PERCENT OF THE WORLD'S WASTE.

9 SQUARE MILES OF RURAL LAND IS TURNED OVER TO DEVELOPMENT EVERY DAY.

THE HOLE IN THE OZONE LAYER HAS BEEN MEASURED UP TO 11 MILLION SQUARE MILES! AND PEOPLE SAY WE SHOULDN'T BE CONCERNED ABOUT GLOBAL WARMING. . . .

9,000 U.S. NATIVE PLANTS AND ANIMALS ARE AT RISK OF EXTINCTION.

WHY AREN'T WE RAISING U.S. FUEL ECONOMY STANDARDS THAT COULD SAVE MORE THAN 2 MILLION BARRELS OF OIL A DAY? I GUESS CONGRESS DOESN'T WANT TO UPSET THE AUTO INDUSTRY.

ELECTION COUNTDOWN
JULY/AUGUST:
CONVENTION SEASON

Logistically, Boston would have been the easiest city for the first annual Peace Party Convention, but it was already hosting the Democratic National Convention during the last week of July. So we moved southeast just a bit and held ours on the beach in Plymouth near the site where the Pilgrims first landed.[76] I tried to block out the fact that the Sagamore Bridge was only a few miles away.

The normal pomp and circumstance of such an event didn't apply to our "Peace Party Party," which actually ended up more like a rave than a national political convention. Janine created amazing compilation CDs—each song bringing cheers from the crowd and building on the song before it. We had invited all the Larry/Beth volunteers and told them to bring their friends. Plus, every Peace Party candidate from across the country was in attendance. The crowd spilled out from under several tents onto the beach.

"I'm guessing four thousand people," Beth said. "It's incredible."

---

[76]They really landed in Provincetown, I know, but they settled in Plymouth and that's what ended up going down in the history books.

I hated to interrupt the festivities with my "acceptance" speech, but knew it had to be done. "Testing one, two . . . testing."

I spoke about the issues we'd been focusing on for months, but mostly I thanked all these committed, passionate people for their time and support. *They* were the ones changing the world, and they knew it too.

Four thousand people—give or take—cheered and partied into the night.

· · ·

A few days later, Beth and I decided to sneak into the Democratic National Convention downtown to check out some of the competition.

It was as radically different from ours as you could get.

How are you supposed to believe a party that says it's for the people, when its national convention is sponsored by corporations?

The Fleet Center showcased so many corporate logos, you'd think the Democrats were playing professional sports.[77] In my mind, I ran through the speech I'd given a few nights before: *I don't want to vote for a candidate who's endorsed by a corporation, do you? I want to vote for someone who's* fighting *corporate greed, not sucking up to it.*

The nametags might as well have read HELLO, MY NAME IS _____, CORPORATE LACKEY AND PUPPET FOR _____.

---

[77]And we all know how *that's* been ruined by greed.

FILL IN THE BLANK. But weren't conventions created so delegates could come together and discuss ways to help *constituents*? (Or was I still being naive?)

Of course, the Republicans were just as bad. I'd read about some Congressional member's blatant pimping at the Republican National Convention in 2000. He didn't even try to hide the fact that he was offering special-interest lobbyists different "packages," charging from fifteen to a hundred thousand dollars for private meetings with the powers that be. It used to be that when politicians sold the public down the river it was behind closed doors. Now they were screwing us right before our eyes. All I could think of was Shemp from the Three Stooges going "nyaaah, nyaaah!" to the guys who chased him around the warehouse.[78]

"Do they think we're blind?" Beth asked. "Or just incredibly stupid?"

"This is what we get when only a handful of people vote. We're paying the price for years of inaction. It just means more work now, that's all."

"You're such an optimist. People don't give up this kind of power without a fight."

We took our seats with the Massachusetts delegates, flashing passes two ex-Democratic interns had given us. The lineup of speakers was about as interesting as widgets going by on a conveyor belt.

---

[78]Don't get me started on a Curly vs. Shemp vs. Joe vs. Curly Joe debate. Believe it or not, I'm even too angry to go there.

"God, they're insufferable. I feel like I'm in a death chamber being smothered with rhetoric gas," I said.

Beth agreed. "I'm imagining them with tattoos and nipple rings underneath their suits. It's the only way I can bear it."

We got into an animated discussion about the electoral college with the guy sitting next to us. I told him that our rich, white, land-owning founding fathers hadn't trusted blacks, women, the poor, or the young enough to let them vote, so they set up the current system.[79] He said many people didn't go to the polls on election day because they already knew how their state's electoral votes would be cast. Beth argued that even though the system no longer worked, it would never be repealed because of the way it favored smaller states. Our private discussion was the only interesting part of the afternoon.

It was just a matter of time before our enthusiasm attracted a security person. When he realized who Beth and I were, he tried to escort us out.

"We have passes," I said. "And every right to be here."

"We're not here to speak," Beth added. "Just to listen."

"Out!" The guard summoned four others to usher us toward the exit.[80]

Was the system so afraid of dissenting opinions that they'd violate someone's civil rights? It suddenly became not

---

[79]The Fifteenth, Nineteenth, Twenty-fourth, and Twenty-sixth Amendments fixed those omissions much later. I told you I was paying attention in class while I was doodling.

[80]Now I know how Ralph Nader felt when they wouldn't even let him *watch* the Bush/Gore debates at UMass back in 2000. Let's face it, for a democratic country, we've been downright hostile to third-party candidates for years.

only necessary but important to stay. Beth and I dug our heels in and grabbed the rail for support. We kicked; we screamed.

We were arrested.[81]

The next day, our photos graced the front page of every major newspaper.

Unfortunately, they were mug shots.

. . .

The charges against Beth and me for trespassing at the Democratic National Convention had been dropped after much public outcry from the country's teens. Kids were getting more vocal and organized, placing pressure on their representatives in Washington to approve the Twenty-eighth Amendment. Both the Democratic and Republican National Committees filed briefs with the U.S. Supreme Court decrying the illegitimacy of my campaign.[82] None of the legal brouhaha interested me; as far as I was concerned, it had nothing to do with the issues at hand.

The media all but canonized the Democratic candidate after he won his party's nomination, and although the president still enjoyed a favorable approval rating, the pundits forecasted a real fight between them.

During the hottest days of summer, Tim and I pretty much had headquarters to ourselves while the other staffers took

---

[81]I could almost see Thoreau smiling from the heavens as I took his theory of civil disobedience to heart.

[82]The Supreme Court—you used to think they were impartial, right? For me, finding out those judges were political puppets too was the saddest part of the 2000 election.

the plum outside assignments. We'd work on the campaign, then cruise the Web for fun. (Tim's favorite hobby? Hacking onto the waiting list for the new Sony Play Station, then adding his friends' names to the top of the list.) I also used the time to catch up on my much-neglected ethology reading. The dog-eat-dog world of politics only fueled my interest in the animal kingdom.

One morning I was sitting alone reading and eating a bowl of raspberries when Beth shuffled into the office. The strap of her bathing suit peeked out from underneath her shirt. She held out the current *People* magazine announcing their "50 Most Beautiful People in the World."

"I can almost empathize with the whole celebrity-worship thing you had going." She turned to page fifty-seven—a full-color photo of Simon flashing a brilliant smile and six-pack abs.

"I knew they had talked to him," she said, "but did he have to pose with no shirt on?"

I held the magazine up to the light, squinting at the rippled muscles on the page. "Did they airbrush this?"

She shook her head. "No, that's all him."

I had to admit, the guy looked good.

"This is everything we're against," Beth said. "I'm so embarrassed."

"I know. Superficial and degrading."[83]

She tossed it into the trash. "You want to go to the beach?"

I threw my book in my bag and headed to Crane's with Beth.

---

[83]Had the magazine even *considered* me?

I couldn't remember how long it had been since I'd had a day to do absolutely nothing. The sand, the sun, and the waves seemed miraculous—here to be enjoyed with no fuss or fanfare. I'd been working such long hours I'd forgotten to schedule time for what connected me most to my life—nature. As Beth and I dove into the surf, I thought about my platform point suggesting every citizen spend a few hours a day outside. Was it dumb to think the world might have many fewer problems that way? Hey, it worked for Thoreau.

Tomorrow Peter, Simon, Beth, and I would fly to Michigan and Illinois for more campaigning, but for now I covered my face with my baseball cap—possession #57—and let myself fall asleep in the sunshine.

• • •

When we returned to our neighborhood that evening, the familiar sight of camera crew and reporters lined the street.

"What now?" I asked. "Can't we take a day off?"

But as I looked more closely, I saw Simon posing on the front lawn of Beth's parents' house.

"Is that a cricket bat?" I asked.

Beth cradled her head in her hands. "He's going to be unbearable."

I told her she could stay at my house, and she looked like she was considering it.[84]

---

[84]Please say yes. Choose me over one of the most beautiful people in the world, I dare you.

"No, I have to deal with this sooner or later." She got out of the car and cut through my yard to avoid the masses.

During the campaign, I'd seen firsthand how much Beth and Simon cared for each other. But I knew Beth well enough to know the scale of the relationship was now tipping toward the negative.

The next morning, the four of us left for the airport before dawn. When I checked out Simon and Beth at the ticket counter, they looked pensive and subdued.

• • •

Three days, thirty stops. By the time we finished supporting a Peace Party candidate at a hospice in Ann Arbor, emotions were frayed. When our motel lost the reservation to Beth and Simon's room, Simon launched into an embarrassing tirade. He and Beth eventually found a room at a bed and breakfast a few blocks away. While Peter ordered takeout, I checked our Web site.

Although the campaign's momentum defied anyone's expectations—especially most adults'—there were plenty of people eager to share their opposing views on our bulletin boards. I welcomed the chance to discuss the issues but was hurt when some people suggested that criticizing our country was unpatriotic. I remembered a Woody Guthrie tape my mother had played over and over in the car when I was young. *"This land is your land. This land is my land. . . ."* She used to sing it with gusto as I bounced in my car seat. I still couldn't hear that song without getting a lump in my throat, and not just from the memories of my mom. I loved this country from the ground up—literally—and was disappointed others didn't realize my actions and words were rooted in devotion.

When I checked the e-mail, I discovered that betagold had gotten ahold of my personal e-mail address.

WELL, LARRY, I WAS GETTING BORED WITH THE WEB SITE AND THOUGHT I'D CONTACT YOU DIRECTLY. HOW'S IT GOING ON THE CAMPAIGN TRAIL? ARE PEOPLE IN THE MIDWEST AS NICE AS THEY SAY?

I scrolled down, in no mood for betagold's chitchat.

THIS IS A WARNING, LARRY. PLEASE TAKE ME SERI-OUSLY. YOU'RE IN OVER YOUR HEAD. WITHDRAW BEFORE YOU GET HURT. I'M ONLY TRYING TO HELP YOU. YOUR PAL, BETAGOLD

The e-mail confused me. Was this a threat, or was she trying to warn me? Was she deflecting attention away from herself? And how did she get my new e-mail address? I called Tim back at headquarters.

"This is turning into a geek tragedy," he said. "I have no idea how she's doing this. But have no fear: Lord High Fixer is here."

By the time I hung up, Tim assured me he'd get to the bottom of things.

Late that night, I was awakened by a key turning in the motel room door. Like an animal on alert, I jumped out of bed, full of the same fear I'd had that night in Boulder.

Peter bounded into the room instead.

"I've been in the restaurant watching the news," he said. "You'll never guess."

I begged him just to tell me.

He shook his head no. "Come on, guess."

"Okay, let's see. The *Enquirer* just hit the stands and I'm a gay albino with ties to the Mafia?"

"Very funny. Are you ready?"

Please don't let this be too mean-spirited. Please let it be something that won't derail us permanently.

"The Greens and the Reform candidates are throwing in the towel. They're telling their followers to support us instead."

"What?!"

"They've been trailing us in the polls since the primaries. They've used up all their resources. Do you know what this means? Probably another three or four percentage points!"

I tried to process the information. Part of me felt bad these candidates were dropping out. I agreed with them on several issues, and let's face it, we all were breaking new ground trying to dismantle the two-party system. I felt as if we were almost on the same team.

"They'll have to let us into the debates now. You have more than 15 percent in the polls. We can finally have a national audience! This is the big leagues, buddy!"

We'd been fantasizing about the debates for months, but now the thought of standing on stage before an audience of forty million television viewers was intimidating, to say the least. I dialed Beth's cell phone—busy. Simon's too. I threw on my clothes and told Peter I had to tell Beth. He offered to call me a cab, but I chose to walk. I headed into the darkness.

The presidential debates! No karaoke machines, no gimmicks, just three people and their ideas for a better country.[85] My initial nervousness began to transform into excitement. I wanted to hear the other candidates answer probing questions, wanted to hear them talk about their promises versus their records. As I walked the empty streets the few blocks to Beth's, I tried to anticipate what her reaction would be.

When I felt the hairs on the back of my neck stand up, I wondered if I should have taken Peter up on his offer for a cab. The bed and breakfast was nearby, but this was a city I didn't know. My fugitive antennae kicked in, and my fear increased. I turned to look over my shoulder; sure enough, a car with dimmed lights was right behind me, cruising slowly.

I started to run, turning left toward the main road. Behind me, I heard the car speed up.

The last thing I remember when the car hit me was the beauty of the Ann Arbor sky.

---

[85]The debates are monitored by a supposedly independent group called the Commission of Presidential Debates, which consists of two ex-Democratic and Republican Party chiefs. They say a candidate needs at least 15 percent of the electorate's support in the opinion polls before he or she can take part in the televised debates. Kind of a catch-22—how are you supposed to get 15 percent of the vote if they won't let you debate? Doesn't sound too independent to me.

When I woke up, the first face I saw was Beth's. "You can't do this to me again—you can't!" Her face was ruddy and her eyes swollen.

Too groggy to answer, I swiveled my head to the other side of the bed in time to watch Peter shaking the doctor's hand.

"You've got a fractured femur," Peter said. "You'll be here for another few days, then six weeks on crutches. You were lucky."

"I don't feel too lucky."

"Janine hasn't stopped calling. She'll be here tomorrow first thing," Peter said.

He handed me a plastic cup with a straw. After a few sips, I found enough of my voice to ask what happened.

"Hit and run," Beth said.

The scene immediately came back to me. "It was a black sedan." Then I rattled off the number of the license plate.

"Oh my God." She ransacked her bag for a pen. "Did you see them?"

"Two men. They were following me with their lights off until I turned the corner. They hit the gas—then me."

"The police wanted to talk to you after you woke up. I was

hoping they were wrong about this." When Peter hurried out of the room, I turned back to Beth.

"I knew this wasn't an accident," Beth said. "I just knew it."

"Where's Simon?"

She gathered the piles of used tissues from the bed. "We broke up."

I tried to reach for her hand, but my arm felt like it weighed a thousand pounds. "What happened?"

"Oh, the groupies, *People* magazine, the way he yelled at that motel clerk last night." She tossed the pile of tissues into the basket. "That and the fact that I'm in love with you."[86]

I didn't care how sore my muscles were, I willed my body toward her. We held each other amidst the tubes and bandages. Although my limbs pulsed with pain, what I felt in my body most strongly was happiness.

"I don't want to get in the way of you and Janine," she said. "I'd rather wait than fight with another woman over a guy. I hate that. It's degrading for everyone."

Then silence. Lots of it.

"It's not like I'm asking you to make a decision between us today." Beth's words said one thing, her expression another. The look on her face could only be called expectant.

"I can't do this now," I said. "I'm barely conscious."

"I know. I'm sorry." I could see the tumblers click as she changed the subject. "Who would do this to you?" she finally asked.

---

[86]Warning: This conversation brought to you courtesy of your morphine drip.

"Oh, I don't know—who have we pissed off in the past few months?"

"Let's see." Beth began to brighten. "The Republicans, the Democrats, greedy CEOs, every soccer mom who wants to keep driving an SUV, every politician who doesn't want to change the campaign finance laws . . ."

I held myself back from adding to her list.

"You don't think betagold had anything to do with this, do you?" she asked.

I told her about yesterday's e-mail.

"I already gave her name to the police," Beth said. "They're checking her out now."

"I don't think betagold's capable of attempted murder, do you?"

Beth's cell rang; she moved to the corner of the room and took the call. I slipped back onto the pillow, exhausted.

"That was Simon. He wanted to make sure you're okay."

I nodded, feeling sleepy from the drugs.

When I woke up again, it was the next day. Peter sat in the chair beside me, his feet on my bed.

"Josh van Winkle, welcome back."

If I didn't get to the bathroom soon, I was going to explode. I made the trip of my own volition—if you don't count the crutches—then dove back into bed.

"I'm starving," I said.

"That's a good sign." He buzzed for the nurse.

"Did I miss anything?"

"Beth's on a rampage to find out who did this. The license

153

plate came back as a rental to a guy with a fake ID. Tracy Hawthorne's totally clean. The police are on it, though."

The thought that the hit-and-run was a deliberate attempt on my life made me feel like never getting out of bed again.

Peter leaned back in his chair and grinned.

"What are you so happy about?" I asked.

"Well, while you were sleeping, there was ONE thing that happened."

"Please don't make me guess, I'm begging you."

He snapped open the newspaper folded on his lap. 28TH AMENDMENT PASSED 51 TO 49. 18-YEAR-OLDS CAN BE PRESIDENT!

I bolted upright. "That's one of those fake newspapers, right? You had it made at a joke shop downtown?"

"Wrong!" Peter could barely contain himself. "The wheels were already in motion, but after the attempt on your life the outcry was so loud the amendment sailed right through the states too."

"It's impossible," I said. "Please tell me you're kidding."

"The reporters are three blocks deep outside, waiting to talk to you."

Beth entered the room quietly, followed by Janine. The two of them seemed as shocked as I was.

"Can you do this?" Beth asked. "Because now is the perfect time to back out if you want to."

For a minute there, I couldn't tell if she was talking about our relationship or the election.

"It's now or never," Janine added. "You have to decide."

Backing out is something I have never been good at.[87] But the idea that I could possibly WIN and become president filled me with such dread, I felt that a lifetime of bedsores and hospital food would actually be more enjoyable. Not because I didn't believe in the issues but because the obstacles and resistance from others trying to protect the status quo seemed insurmountable. I mean, someone had just tried to kill me! Was there a traitor in our midst? Would he or she try to hurt me again? Could I bypass the press corps outside so I could pop home to Bloomingdale's and run all this by Mom?

No one on the campaign knew the laundry list of doubts that kept me up most nights. Who was I to think I'd run the country any better than professional politicians? What skills did *I* have to offer? What finally got me to sleep in those early hours was thinking about Rosa Parks or Cesar Chavez, regular citizens who probably thought they had nothing to offer the world either—until one day when challenging the status quo suddenly seemed more important than upholding it. Their efforts may have seemed inconsequential at the time, but ended up shifting our society forever.

Did I have it in me to try? To risk everything for possibly a better way?

I stared at Beth's and Janine's optimistic faces but I knew the decision was ultimately my own. I ripped the I.V. from my arm.

"We're running," I said. "And we're going to win."

---

[87]Unless, of course, you count pretending you had killed yourself.

PART FOUR

"It is we who have squandered the public trust. We who
have, time and again, in full public view placed our
personal and partisan interests before the national interest,
earning the public's contempt for our poll-driven policies,
our phony posturing, the lies we call spin, and the damage
control we substitute for progress. It is we who are the
defenders of a campaign finance system that is nothing
less than an elaborate influence-peddling scheme in which
both parties conspire to stay in office by selling the
country to the highest bidder."

Senator John McCain

ELECTION COUNTDOWN
SEPTEMBER:
LEGAL AT LAST

If you took all the Larry frenzy after betagold outed me and multiplied it by a thousand, *that's* the kind of pressure I felt now. I told myself it was no big deal if we lost—we had been planning on losing up until a few weeks ago. But thousands of kids were becoming politically involved every day, and I refused to let them down.

For nine months I'd been complaining that the mainstream media hadn't covered our campaign, but the current attention felt more like a searchlight shining down on someone trying to escape from prison. We now had a press bus that followed us along the campaign trail. I used every opportunity to discuss the Peace Party platform, but even a stimulation junkie like me got tired of such a rigorous interview and travel schedule. (One thing I didn't complain about was a guest appearance on *Saturday Night Live* in a political debate sketch. *That* was hilarious.)

The real presidential debates were next month; I tried not to obsess about them, but of course I did. And not having Simon around to strategize was a real letdown.

He'd gone back to Harvard for the fall semester, but I found myself calling him late at night with questions of strategy and policy.[88] Judging by the variety of women answering his phone, he wasn't wasting any time getting over Beth.

And for once, I found myself faced with two women who wanted me. Me! If my time weren't being consumed by a presidential campaign, I might even have a chance to revel in such unexpected good fortune.

Of course, our entire campaign hinged on me being eighteen, an event that finally occurred in September. I spent the day outlining each year of my life, going back to age two and a half and analyzing all the things I'd learned.[89] I plotted it all in a colorful Venn diagram that I tucked into my notebook.

The orthopedic surgeon vetoed Peter's idea for a bowling party, thank God, so Janine and Beth planned a dinner celebration at a Mexican restaurant, complete with a decrepit birthday sombrero.[90]

Knowing how much noise we would probably make, Beth had wisely requested a private room in the back of the restaurant. Peter made an embarrassingly candid toast, and Tim and Lisa sang a much-too-loud and nasty limerick they'd composed that afternoon. When Janine got them to sit down, I was grateful, if only for a moment.

---

[88]Or just to have someone to recite the Dead Parrot sketch with.

[89]You do that on birthdays too, right?

[90]Which thankfully covered the worst haircut I'd ever received in my life—a boys' regular from a barbershop on the road in Des Moines. I hate to admit it, but when I obsessed about the nationally televised debates, half the time I was worrying if my hair would grow out by then.

"Well, Larry," she said. "We thought the party might need some entertainment."

Beth pulled back the curtain leading to the next room and made way for a tall, middle-aged belly dancer.

Everyone at the table turned to me and laughed.

I tried to smile good-naturedly but felt my cheeks burn. My shyness soon transformed itself to horror when the woman turned on her boom box and began to gyrate in front of me.

Beth and Janine couldn't contain themselves; they stood across the room and howled.[91]

"Are we torturing you?" Beth asked. "We all thought you needed a little levity."

"Isn't this more appropriate for a Middle Eastern restaurant?" I asked.

Janine laughed. "I thought you were big on diversity—come on!"

Have you ever had one of those times when you pretend to be happy because you're supposed to be, because you know that people you love have put so much effort into doing something nice for you, but all you really want is for everyone to just go away? I smiled, I laughed, but my mind was elsewhere.

I tried to focus on the woman's dancing skills, but I had made so many speeches about the Middle East lately it was impossible not to watch her and think about the atrocities being committed in her part of the world. I made a mental note

---

[91] Why aren't they fighting over me? Why are they *bonding*?

to ask the president about the peace process when I saw him next month.

The woman jangled her bracelets in my face, snapping me out of my reverie.[92] I knew no one, let alone I, could make a dent in international affairs tonight so I set my mind on a different problem—the Janine/Beth debate.

I'd been playing emotional Ping-Pong since Beth had broken up with Simon. Beth/Janine. Janine/Beth. Because of all the miles we were logging, tonight was the first time in a month the three of us had been in the same city at the same time. I found myself in the enviable/impossible position of choosing between them.

After twenty minutes and much applause, the woman packed up her boom box and left. I approached Janine and Lisa.

"Nice surprise," I said. "Thanks."

"Tim wanted to order a stripper," Lisa said. "You should be grateful."

Janine grabbed her bag and gave me a hug. "I'm taking the eleven o'clock flight out of Logan. Lisa's giving me a ride."

As if on cue, Lisa made her way around the table saying goodbye.

"What are you talking about? I thought you were staying till tomorrow."

She nodded at Beth across the room. "I know you'd rather

---

[92]I'm not the only person analyzing foreign policy while watching a belly dancer, am I?

162

be with Beth on your birthday. It kills me, but I'm not going to stay and make a scene."

"No, you're wrong—"

"Then you *do* want me?"

"I . . . I don't know what I want. This is new terrain for me."

"Then let me make it easy for you. I'll see you in a few weeks, okay? Call me."

"Janine, no—"

She kissed me goodbye, then slipped out the door with Lisa.

Hel-lo? Why had I thought it would be *my* choice who I ended up with tonight? I stared at Beth across the room, jumping up and down with excitement as she talked to Billy. She could hardly be called a consolation prize. I limped my way over to her as the party broke up.

Since Beth hadn't returned to Brown this semester, she was staying with her parents on the rare occasions we weren't on the road. I hoped she'd come back to my house afterward; she eagerly said yes.

As I maneuvered my crutches up the front stairs, I noticed Peter camped out in the living room. Wasn't it time for him to go to bed?

But no, he sat with us pontificating about the next few months, so crucial to the campaign. I gave him several hints to leave the room, but he didn't.

After half an hour, Beth stood up.

"Where are you going?" I asked.

"I'm so sleep deprived, I can't keep my eyes open."

"Come on, it's early." I hobbled to the back door after her.

She pulled me close and kissed me. "I'm not playing second string to Janine—I know you wanted to be with her tonight."

"No I didn't!"

"I told you back in the hospital—it's not my style to fight with another girl over a guy. Waste of time." She kissed me again. "Happy birthday."

She closed the door behind her.

I opened it again. "You two did this on purpose, didn't you? Some sick birthday joke? He's an adult now, let's torture him."

"Night, Josh."

When I returned to the living room, Peter tried to contain his laughter.

"It's not funny," I said.

"I didn't say anything."

"I'm eighteen, and I feel about twelve."

"You should feel lucky two terrific women care so much about you."

"Yeah, care enough to leave." I told Peter I was going to bed.

I stared at myself in the bathroom mirror for a long time. I was eighteen at last. Old enough to vote, to have a say in things. Talk about the proverbial grown-ups' table. And here I was, broken leg, the most bizarre haircut of my life, guacamole all over my T-shirt, and let's not forget the frosting on the (birthday) cake—someone had recently tried to kill me. But all I could think about was Janine and Beth.

What if they hadn't beaten me to the punch tonight? What if I did have to choose between them? For months, my mind had been overflowing with the details of the campaign, barely giving me any time to listen to the tiny voice inside me guiding me through this thorny girlfriend decision. Yet as I stood before the mirror now, strains of that voice became clearly audible. I knew which one I loved more.

"Josh?" Peter appeared in the doorway in his robe. "Happy birthday, buddy."

He hugged me, then shuffled down the hall.

I shut off the light knowing I wouldn't have time to sort through and finalize the Janine/Beth triangle until after the election. I headed to my room alone.

Some things never change.

ELECTION COUNTDOWN

OCTOBER:

THE PRESIDENTIAL DEBATES

Even without me, the debates were a thorn in the side of the other candidates. They'd never admit it, but all the hemming and hawing about venue, format, and questions could be traced back to fear. Not fear of speaking to an audience of tens of millions of people, but trepidation about how much was at stake. One misstep, one wishy-washy answer and you were mercilessly crucified by the pundits seconds after the debate ended.

I tried to negotiate for tougher questions, even suggesting that consumer advocates and regular citizens sit on the panel. No go. The powers that be didn't want any surprises.

The Peace Party team spent a lot of time debating among ourselves. Should we use some of the theatrics that had gained us notoriety several months back? Should we be on the offensive from the get-go or should we present our own proposals without talking about the other candidates' weaknesses?

We eventually decided the situation demanded a polite, serious demeanor and vetoed the pith helmet. (It's a jungle out there.) I was also grateful when the doctor okayed me to lose the crutches.

Peter stopped me on my way to the auditorium. "You're kidding, right? You're not wearing that.".

I looked down at my MEAN PEOPLE SUCK T-shirt. "If I get a suit, a tie, and dress shoes, I'll be at more than seventy-five possessions. I don't want to go through that again."

"You can trade in a few CDs and books," he said. "You can donate the suit to charity tomorrow. But you are *not* wearing a T-shirt to a presidential debate."

"It's my good luck shirt. I've had it for years."[93]

A glimpse of the old Peter emerged. "Josh Swensen, go back to your room right now and change."

"What am I, five?"

He blocked my path to the hall. I'm sure any student in Psych 101 would say this power struggle was our way of dealing with the monumental stress of the occasion, and they'd probably be right. I stubbornly bulldozed past my stepfather to the hall beyond.

• • •

After weeks of negotiating, it had been decided that the first debate would be held at the University of Wisconsin. As I entered the auditorium, I was shocked by the rows of empty seats.

"I thought we agreed to have an audience—"

---

[93]It was also what I was wearing on my last vision quest when Beth paid me that little visit. I mean, come on!

"Last-minute change," the producer said. "We're doing a tape delay too."

"What? This was supposed to be live!"

She told me to get over it.

It didn't take long to realize what Peter told me later, that so many of the people who had originally gotten tickets were students, and neither of the other candidates wanted a youthful crowd. Instead, I found myself face-to-face with several unsmiling middle-aged panelists.

I had never met either candidate before; I wiped my hands against my T-shirt to get rid of the sweat. Both men were friendly, even if they did seem amused at having to deal with someone my age.

"I'm just kind of wondering why we're having this in an auditorium if there aren't any *people* here," I said.

"'Just kind of wondering'?" the president asked.

I tried not to let them throw me off track. I went for some levity. "I mean, if you two were afraid of having actual people, we could've just used a television studio."

They both laughed, and the producer told us to take our places on the stage. So much for bowling them over with my personality.

When the moderator asked the first question, my knees almost buckled.

They had changed the questions.

I did my best to keep up, but the topics were so vague I never would have agreed to them. It took all my willpower to focus.

Listening to the other candidates speak to the watered-down issues, I didn't know how anyone could distinguish one from the other. Their platitudes and generalities were completely interchangeable. The whole exercise reminded me of the teacher's voice in a Charlie Brown cartoon—*waah, waah, waah*—an insufferable drone.

When it was my turn, the moderator turned to me. "Mr. Swensen, you have three minutes to rebut the president."

I spent the first few seconds of my allotted time staring at the empty auditorium seats. They seemed an apt metaphor for both candidates' lifeless campaigns. This whole thing had been rigged; everyone was in on the joke but me. How could I possibly change a system so deeply rooted and self-serving?

Then the two candidates winked at each other.

My original plan had been to only talk about Peace Party initiatives. But those condescending winks kicked me into attack mode pretty quickly.

Mr. President, let's talk about your administration's report card. As of today, the stock market has lost $4.8 trillion since your inauguration. There's been a 43 percent jump in unemployment. Forty-three percent of the tax cut you pushed through went to the country's wealthiest 1 percent. Oh, and let's not forget invading another country without provocation or the blessing of the U.N. Didn't you run on a platform of a "humble foreign policy"? Your reasons for invading Iraq were to find weapons of mass destruction. As of now, we haven't found a one. You followed that up by awarding more than $1.7 billion of government contracts to your corporate cronies. I guess if someone had to manage the Iraqi oilfields, it might as well be your friends.

You say your Homeland Security Act is the answer to keeping our country safe. But did you tell us what was in the fine print? Corporate loopholes and handouts, not to mention that high schools had to hand over the names and phone numbers of every student to the military. Schools that refused because they valued their students' privacy would lose valuable federal funding. How does cutting school budgets help to fight terrorism?

And how about the Information Awareness Office—didn't you read any George Orwell when you were my age? What you've created is scarier than anything in his fiction. Every credit card purchase, phone call, magazine subscription, e-mail, video rental, and bank deposit can go into a centralized Pentagon database. Since when is the ordinary citizen the enemy?

Am I the only one who thinks the foxes are guarding the henhouse here? We've got two millionaires in the White House—is that a fair representation of the average American? Are you looking out for us or for your bigwig friends?

The laws you put into place during your Administration will affect us for years. When the Iroquois used to make decisions, they asked themselves how the result would affect the next seven generations. Has anyone been thinking that far ahead?

Under your helm, our country has seen unprece-
dented budget deficits, economic downfalls, as well as
war, yet you've taken 166 vacation days at your ranch
while the average American gets 16 days off a year.
People have said I haven't taken the job of president seri-
ously enough—have you?

The silence was deafening.

The president flexed his hands repeatedly by his sides. His buddies who owned the large media corporations had been keeping a lid on many of these stories in exchange for lenient FCC regulations, but he knew everything I said was true. If the auditorium had been full of students, the place would have jumped to its feet. Instead, a group of horrified Brooks Brothers panelists shook their heads in dismay.

The moderator told the president he had a thirty-second rebuttal. The president didn't denounce anything I said, just looked me dead in the eye.

"Son, I want to know why you live in this country if it's so bad."

I knew I wasn't supposed to answer his rebuttal, but leaned forward anyway. "Why would I leave, when I can work toward fixing something I believe in? Isn't that what you adults always say kids should be doing?"

When the moderator objected to my breach of protocol, the president waved him off as if I could never say anything of any consequence. It was at that point that I realized the president had a strand of toilet paper stuck to the bottom of his left shoe. I wondered if his Secret Service agents had missed it or if they were letting him walk around like that on purpose. Either way, it was beautiful.

For the next question, it was the Democrats' turn to peddle their wares. The candidate talked about how revitalized the Democratic Party was, how it represented the "average American." When it was my turn, I didn't waste a second of my three minutes.

I'm so glad to hear you say the Democratic Party is back in business. This certainly is news to me as well as to millions of other Americans. But when you look at the facts, your record is just as bad as the current Administration's.

The environment? When the last Democrat was in office, he never introduced the Kyoto Protocol into the Senate for ratification.[94] He didn't sign the 1997 Mine Ban Treaty. He didn't force Detroit to improve cars' fuel efficiency.

Campaign finance reform? The last Democratic president took as much money in corporate kickbacks as the Republicans did; in fact, he expanded the soft money loophole! And if you look at the voting record of the Democrats in the House, most of them have been voting along with the Republicans on major issues right down the line. We don't have a two-party system! We have one party—the Suck Up to Big Business Party. Where does

---

[94]An international agreement to reduce global warming signed by almost every country except us.

the "average person" fit in? As someone sitting by on the sidelines while politicians loot the land?

If the Democrats were really revitalized, why didn't they insist the trillion-dollar national surplus be spent on health care for the forty-four million Americans who don't have it instead of refunds to the wealthiest 1 percent? The minimum wage hasn't been raised since 1997, but you sat on the sidelines while this Administration handed out billions of dollars in corporate rebates. Why did you let them? Why didn't you refuse to spend hundreds of billions of dollars on starting a war a world away and instead focus our money and energies here? Why are you letting this Administration commit billions of dollars to a missile shield system that even they acknowledge doesn't work?

No wonder you people are so threatened by the Peace Party. We're what the Democratic Party used to be—idealistic and energized. Listening to all the people at our rallies just makes you realize how much you sold out!

I'm sorry, but have you guys forgotten who elected you? As I've said throughout my campaign all along—you work for us, remember?

I was *pumped*.

The producer yelled "cut" at the end of the debate, and I approached both candidates to shake their hands. But they turned their backs on me and quickly left the stage.[95]

---

[95]This country was founded on dissent and the exchange of differing views. Cut me some slack here!

Peter met me backstage and gave me a big hug. "You knocked it out of the park, Josh. I can't wait to hear the pundits on this one."

We hurried back to our rooms at the hostel to watch the debate on tape delay. When *Will and Grace* came on instead of the scheduled debate, Peter called the producer's cell phone. I could hear him screaming from the next room.

Then Peter plopped down on the bottom bunk, took off his baseball cap, and rubbed his head.

"Technical difficulties. They say the entire tape is scratched."

"That's crap," Beth said. "They don't want the voters to hear Josh exposing the other candidates for who they are."

"We haven't gained an inch," I added. "Even with the amendment, they're disenfranchising us the same way they disenfranchise every other American."

"Of course, there are technical difficulties sometimes," Peter said. "I had several close calls shooting commercials in my past life."

Beth nailed her can of soda into the trash so hard the wastebasket fell over. "I can't believe you're sticking up for them!"

Peter reached into the pocket of his jacket. "I'm not defending them. I'm just saying I always had a backup plan." He popped out the tape from his recorder.

"No," I stammered. "Not the whole debate?"

"I had to shoot it from backstage and hide it when Security came by, so the quality's not too good. But I got all of it."

174

I grabbed my laptop and hooked it up to the recorder. Peter was right; the image quality was just okay, but the audio was clear as a bell. I downloaded the debate onto the Larry Web site. Lisa called the press to alert them to the bootleg. Within the hour, every major network had interrupted their programming to broadcast the debate. A reporter for CNN interviewed the show's producer to comment on the so-called technical difficulties; the poor woman looked like she needed a straitjacket, she was flailing around with so much anger.

For once I had to admit I didn't mind the media focusing on non-issues. The clip the networks played over and over again was Peter zooming in on the toilet paper stuck to the president's shoe.

The next day, the pundits and pollsters had me up by 7 percentage points in the polls. Investigative reporters at all the major newspapers began to cover the items I'd raised during the debate. The other two candidates were being asked tougher questions, and their answers were scrutinized for accuracy. Both the Democratic and Republican candidates bowed out of the next two debates, citing scheduling conflicts. I knew they'd rather both wrestle in Jell-O on live TV than subject themselves to another grueling session that actually dealt with something as important as their records.

By all accounts, we had won the battle.

Little did I know we were headed for a war.

. . .

With just a few weeks left until Election Day, our campaign staff kicked into overdrive. Volunteers canvassed neighborhoods by foot and phone. Beth and I made appearances on *Hardball, Crossfire,* and *The O'Reilly Factor*. (What a bunch of negative Johnny Appleseeds *those* guys are.) We garaged the tour bus and flew to several swing states for rallies.[96] And with the thousands of barrels filled with coins from our drop-off points across the country, we had enough funds to run a few crucial ads.

Janine made time in her equally jam-packed schedule to fly out to L.A. to meet us. She deftly helped Tara, the California coordinator, organize our four stops that morning. We made appearances with several other Peace Party candidates, but when Tara suggested that I looked exhausted and should take a break, I took her up on the offer.

Janine, Brady, and I collapsed into the motel room with several cartons of Chinese takeout.

Janine had just filled her plate when Beth barreled through the door.

"I'm sorry to interrupt, but this can't wait," she said. "*Newsweek* and CNN just called. They're going with a story that you have an offshore bank account with $190 million in it."

I grabbed a Peking ravioli. "Yeah, right."

"That's what I said, but they have account numbers, a list of donors—everybody from GE to Ford to Exxon."

---

[96]Due to the Patriot Act, I was stopped at every security checkpoint because of who I was. I'm all for airline security, but I always missed my flight. Gee, I thought by trying to make the country a better place, I *was* being patriotic.

"I'm sure."

"Here are the faxes. The account numbers trace back to our bank in Boston. The correspondence is on our stationery. They have copies of e-mails between you and the CEO of General Motors saying you won't tighten emission standards if you get elected."

"What?" Janine looked as upset as I'd ever seen her. We laid out the documents on the bed and studied them.

"Now are you getting it?" Beth asked. "It's all crap, but the paperwork is completely legit. How did they get your e-mail password or our account numbers? I told you all along, Josh— there's somebody on the inside."

I wanted to block my ears like a little kid. *I'm not listening. I'm not listening.*

I knew the political Attack Machines would do anything to ensure that I failed, especially after the success of the debate. And out of all the scandals that plagued candidates—sexual improprieties, harassment, employing illegal aliens, lying under oath—surely the one that would hit me the hardest would be anything linking me to Big Business.

But everything looked accurate, right down to my messy handwriting. Mixed in with notes I did write to staffers, Peter, and supporters were things I never would have written in a thousand years. I mean, a note to the CEO of Monsanto promising that if elected I'd help him "slide their genetically modified soy and wheat crops on the unsuspecting public"? Were they kidding? When I lived in Boulder, I belonged to a group that spent six months fighting that one particular issue. I would

have preferred a doctored photo of me rehearsing with
'N Sync than this nonsense.

"How did they do it?" Janine asked.

"I'm more concerned with who," Beth said. "It almost doesn't
matter if it's Democrats or Republicans. I just want to know who
gave them access to our files. That's the real betrayal."

"Maybe it's like Watergate and they broke in," Janine
suggested.

"No way. None of the passwords are written down," I
answered.

"Maybe they had that software that records keystrokes. Or
maybe the phones are bugged," Beth said.

"Let's call a meeting in Boston for the morning and fly back
tonight."

I wanted to be in the air and inaccessible when the story
broke. Peter's voice crumbled as I told him the news by phone.

"We're not going to let this get us down, Josh. There have
been obstacles all along the way. We'll get through this."

Janine decided to come back to Boston to help out. Several people on the plane recognized Beth and me; a few shook
our hands.

"Flying coach," one man said. "I guess you *do* practice
what you preach."

"You've got my vote," said another. "I'm tired of these trust
fund men running the show."

"We'll see if they feel that way tomorrow," I whispered to
Beth as we took our seats.

The rest of the flight was turbulent, if only in my mind. Beth hadn't mentioned betagold, but she didn't have to. Her twisted vengeance lay underneath both our thoughts.

I knocked the tray with my knee, causing my little can of tomato juice to sail across the aisle. All I could do was cross my fingers that the American public would hear my side of the story tomorrow and somehow believe me.

They didn't.

ELECTION COUNTDOWN
LAST WEEK IN OCTOBER:
THE FINAL PUSH

The next several days were filled with more questions than I'd answered in my entire life.[97]

I told my side of the story ad nauseam—that the money wasn't mine, that I was being set up, that whoever had done this considered $190 million an investment in maintaining the status quo. The reporters refused to believe anyone would spend that much money just to frame someone. I told them it was a drop in the bucket for most corporate donors, a cost-of-doing-business expense that ensured one of their political puppets got elected instead of me.

Of course, all the protesting in the world couldn't hide the fact that the signature on the account appeared to be mine or that the e-mails to various executives could be traced to the PC I used at campaign headquarters. Even more difficult to refute were the statements of several multi-billion-dollar CEOs who swore I had approached them for donations in exchange for favorable legislation.

After two days of fighting the tide of negative press, I

---

[97]Like an oral version of the SAT, just less fun.

pedaled off to my hole in the woods to weigh my options. Should I withdraw from the ticket and let Beth run alone? Should I go down fighting? Use our last funds for a national ad telling my side of the story?

There was one option I didn't want to think about as I pedaled toward the familiar hideaway. But in the back of my mind, an unforgivable choice kept trying to make itself heard.

You left without a trace before, it said. *You can do it again.*

No, absolutely not. I kept riding.

You could take some of the money. It's in your name; they owe you. You know how to do it. It would be easier this time.

I won't commit pseudocide again. I won't do it to Beth. Or to Peter or Janine. Not to mention the millions of people who believe in what we've been trying to do for ten months.

You don't owe anybody anything. Think about yourself for a change.

I shook my head violently as I rode, trying to make these terrible thoughts disappear. Just a few hundred yards and I'd be safe.

But when I turned the corner toward the trail, cars and trucks filled both sides of the street. How had they found out about this, my one last place of calm on the planet? I tucked my head down and pedaled past the turnoff.

You're nuts if you don't consider it, the voice continued. *They're never going to let you be.*

I headed back to the main road, not sure what I wanted to escape from more—the media spotlight or the voices in my own head.

181

. . .

It got so bad that Peter had to escort me into headquarters every morning. He looked as mad as he'd been in the old days. "Vultures, all of them," he complained.

Janine and Beth were both on computers in the office, scanning files.

"We've been here since 4 A.M.," Beth said. "Still not a clue. Do you think they hacked their way in?"

"Anything's possible. What does Tim say?"

"He's asleep in the hall, something about 'changing phases the hard way.' He was up all night too."

Janine looked weary but optimistic. Knowing her, she would work till we dragged her out of the building kicking and screaming. I knew better than to ask her how it was going; it was a silent Monday.

When Tim woke up and Lisa arrived, we went through every detail of our protocol yet again.

"I think we should stop focusing on who did what and just get on with the damage control," Lisa said. "The election's a week away."

"It's totally foobar," Tim said. "You should just give it up."

Peter disagreed. "I say we hold another press conference, be fresh in the voters' minds."

"The voters still think I screwed them over," I said. "It's going to take more than a press conference to sweep all that hypocrisy under the table."

"We've gone from a high of 27 to 9 percent in the polls," Lisa said.

Beth couldn't control her anger. "The polls are rigged—you know that."

She left the table to take a call on her cell. As the others talked, I kept my eyes on her. I could see the color drain from her face as she spoke.

Beth hung up and nodded for me to join her in the hall.

"You're not going to like this," she said.

"I haven't liked anything since this story broke. Shoot."

"It was Janine."

"Would you stop with that already? I told you it's not her."

Beth didn't look angry, just sad. "Tony traced the Cayman Island documents to the fax in Colorado headquarters. And the e-mails were generated from Janine's computer."

I pulled Beth into the office. "It wasn't Janine!"

"She knew your passwords, she knew our account numbers, she had access to your laptop every time she stayed over."

"You just never got over the fact that—"

"This isn't about you!" She walked over to the documents streaming out of the fax. "Tony's sending over the information. Maybe if you see it in black and white we can move forward."

Page after page, the evidence pointed straight to Janine: phone calls, records, bank statements.

Beth looked over my shoulder as I read. "Oh my God. They found a bank account in Boulder in her name—with almost a million dollars in it."

"We have to give her the benefit of the doubt," I said. "The money could be planted, just like they did with me."

"Okay, but what about this?" She held up a copy of a photograph—Janine and an older woman talking in the lobby of an office building.

The woman was betagold.

My whole body began to shake. "They're probably doctored. With the right software you can manipulate any photograph."

"Tony's got the negative. He's holding it in his hand."

I paced around the room like a cheetah being crated for the zoo. "Maybe Tony's lying."

Beth looked about to cry. "Tony's my cousin, you've known him forever. It's not Tony."

"This must make you happy," I barked. "You've been warning me about Janine all along."

"Of course it doesn't make me happy—she's *my* friend now too!"

I dragged a chair to the corner of the office. No matter how disappointed Beth felt, it was nothing compared to the hurt setting down roots inside me. I thought back to the night of my birthday a few months ago when I stood in front of the bathroom mirror trying to hear my inner voice cast its vote in the Janine/Beth debate. Janine's name was the one I heard when I asked my heart to speak that night. Her betrayal wounded me on so many levels, I had to force myself to breathe.

Beth gently approached my chair. "I'm not saying she was

in it from the beginning, and I'm sure she didn't have anything to do with the hit-and-run."

My mind reeled with a pathetic conspiracy theory: Suppose Janine had met me intentionally in Boulder? Suppose whoever was behind this had been following me for years? Suppose the first girlfriend I ever had in my life was only with me because she'd been paid to be?

I couldn't go there.

"I'm sorry," Beth said. "But we have to get her out—she's in the middle of a strategy meeting."

Tim skidded by with a stack of papers and asked if everything was okay. Beth told him to send Janine over.

"No, let her stay where she is," I said. "I want everyone to hear this."

• • •

Janine was dutifully taking notes, the plastic goldfish glued to the top of her pen bouncing up and down as she wrote. She smiled when she saw me, a grin that quickly dissipated when she registered the look on my face.

I tossed the faxes on the table. "Maybe you want to be the one to spring for lunch today, Janine. I mean, with more than nine hundred thousand dollars in your new savings account, you should be able to afford a few pizzas."

She scanned through the faxes, perplexed; I had temporarily forgotten it was a silent day.

"It's a good thing you can't say anything," I continued.

185

"Because I don't want to hear it." I kicked my chair over, and it slid across the hardwood floor. I faced the others at the makeshift conference table. "Seems Janine here is the one who's been feeding all the info to our opponents. The paper trail leads right back to Colorado." Lisa shook her head as if unwilling to believe it.

Janine wrote furiously on her pad, the fish bobbing for its life. She held up the page. IT WASN'T ME! I SWEAR!

"I knew I shouldn't have trusted you. You came around a little too easily." I picked my chair off the floor and sat next to her. "Pretending to love me—did they pay you to do that too?"

I could see the struggle on her face—defend herself and break her five-year vow of silence or sit there and take it?

She sat there and took it.

And did I give it. I poured on the humiliation full force. I can honestly say I'd never spoken to another person with such anger and hate in my life.

Beth finally interrupted. "That's enough, Josh. Somebody take Janine to the airport."

Lisa grabbed her car keys. Janine left all her folders and notes on the table, taking only her Hello Kitty purse and Brady. As she headed to the door, she turned to face me head-on, tears streaming down her face.

"It wasn't me," she stammered. "But I'll tell the press it was if you want me to."

I waved her off, wishing she had kept her vow of silence so I wouldn't have to hear the sound of her voice breaking.

The press didn't buy it.

Even with Janine admitting the offshore holdings were a hoax, I continued to sink in the polls.[98] Because all the papers described Janine as my girlfriend, the whole thing looked like a ploy: She was sticking up for me to save the election.

Then something even more bizarre began to happen. Once corporate America got wind that I was supposedly taking money from CEOs, other execs wanted in on the action. I began to get several calls a day from businessmen with fat checkbooks thanking me for "finally playing ball." The bastards were hedging their bets, throwing money at me on the slim chance that I'd win or throw my votes toward one of the other candidates. The whole thing seemed so ludicrous, I thought more and more about heading to the Sagamore.

---

[98]Another catch-22: if the press buried the new facts of the story on page forty-seven, how was I supposed to clear my name and start to catch up in the polls again? Throughout the campaign, I'd spoken about how wrong it was for six conglomerates to own almost all the U.S. media outlets. I was now experiencing their corporate wrath and one-sidedness firsthand.

"Okay," Peter said. "We've come up with two good options. You have the final say, but here are the pros and cons."

I shuffled to the kitchen, got a jar of peanut butter from the cupboard, and jabbed a spoon into it.

"Idea number one: we take the money and—"

"We're not taking the money."

"I hear what you're saying, I really do." In an ingrained act of salesmanship, Peter got his own spoon and joined me with the peanut butter. "But the money *is* in your name."

"If we use it, they win, don't you see? If anybody has listened to *one* of my sermons, they'd know I'd never touch a penny. Let them take it back the same way they put it there."

"Okay, we've always been big on the responsibility of voters, right? How disgraceful it is that our country is dead-last in the world in voter turnout?"

I nodded, the spoon locked in place between my teeth.

"We withdraw the money, send checks to our offices around the country, and pay people to vote. Say, a hundred bucks each."

Peter went on to explain that it wouldn't be bribery; we could pay people *after* they voted, not before. "It wouldn't even matter if they voted for us. Just that they voted. We get our staffers handing out hundred-dollar bills, wearing sandwich boards—make it fun. We use their money to bring out the vote. It's perfect."

I thought about the idea; it actually had some merit.

"But I'm not sure it sends the right message. All along I've said that democracy isn't a spectator sport. It's our *duty* to vote." I scooped another dollop of peanut butter. "What else can you think of that's responsible and radical at the same time?"

He tossed his spoon into the sink. "Just trying to make lemonade out of these lemons, Josh. I hate to quit after all the good work we've done."

I agreed with him, but even my overactive mind had struck out on this one.

Peter turned on the kitchen radio to catch NPR describing our "young and passionate campaign staff—interviews with Lisa Carroll and Tim Hawthorne up next." I couldn't bear that they were talking about our campaign as if it were over. As I grabbed the knob and buzzed down the dial, a snippet of Dylan emerged from the speakers. Out of the guy's entire canon of music—hundreds of songs—this was the line that screamed across the room. *"When you ain't got nothing, you got nothing to lose."*

It was a musical coincidence that Janine would have loved.

Ahhh, Janine. I hadn't answered any of her e-mails or phone calls. Surprisingly, the weight of my grief and hurt no longer stemmed from her betrayal but my reaction to it. A week later, I was still horrified by my behavior. No matter what she'd done, humiliating her like that was inexcusable. I'd spent that night sleeping on the cold hard seats of the school bus, too mad at myself to go inside the house. I sat with my flashlight, thumbing through the copy of my previous book until I found the section I was looking for. *But I didn't have to preach to a*

million people to move civilization forward; offering a hungry
person a bowl of soup was contributing too . . . I had been try-
ing to fix the outside world without fixing the inside one first—a
giant mistake.

I read my own words again. Here I was, at the finish line of being the first teenager to run for president and I'd failed. Not failed at running a good campaign, but at being a decent human being. The offshore holdings scandal hadn't blown it, Janine's betrayal hadn't blown it—*I* had. From the beginning I'd run this campaign with respect and honesty for staffers and voters alike. I'd broken that vow when I spoke to Janine so harshly. Whatever happened from here on in, I deserved.

I scanned my Word Search for the Senator Wellstone quote I'd used when I announced my candidacy. *"Let there be no distance between the words you say and the life you live."* The election hadn't even happened yet and I was already a loser.

I put on my jacket and asked Peter if I could borrow his bike.

"We have to decide what we're doing by the morning," he said. "If you don't, I will."

I nodded and headed out the door.

• • •

All the way to Chestnut Hill, I weighed Peter's suggestions. Beth had cornered me the night before, urging us to spend the money on a national ad campaign that underscored the issues we'd raised all year. Simon called from Harvard to suggest that aggressive attacks required aggressive responses. As I coasted down Route 9, I also wondered what the five e-mails from Janine had contained before I had deleted them.

Marlene's face lit up when she saw me enter the makeup department.

"I don't care what the papers say. You get my vote—100 percent."

I thanked her and plopped down on the padded stool.

When she winked, her penciled-in eyebrows didn't move. "Lots of people shopping—you'll get good reception today."

I was happy to hear the news; the last few times I'd come, I'd barely heard anything from Mom at all. I settled in and watched the shoppers buzz by.

"Mom, you obviously know about Janine, about me being framed, about the campaign going right down the toilet. We've got a few options on the table—all of them lousy choices, but still—I have no idea what to do. You're the only one I trust with something this important. Will you help me?"

I gazed up at the fluorescent lights and waited.

And waited.

After about fifteen minutes, I felt like I was sitting in a Bloomingdale's Bermuda Triangle where no instrumentation worked. Women would be chatting, but come to a conversational lull as they approached. Men would flip their cells closed as they entered my periphery. Toddlers would miraculously be soothed and quiet as they moved by the counter.

I was surprised but not despondent.

Until the unthinkable hit me.

She was gone.

I fidgeted on the stool like a two-year-old. "Mom, Mom, Mom," I muttered to myself. "You can't do this to me."

Janine's betrayal was one thing. Losing the trust of millions of Americans who believed in me was another. But having to say goodbye—*real* goodbye, *forever* goodbye—to my mother? That was more than I could bear.

I settled back into the silence of Bloomingdale's as if someone had hit a storewide mute button.

After a few minutes, I did hear a sound.

My own sobbing.

Big racking sobs, accompanied by a runny nose and lots of sniffling.

Marlene scurried toward me with a box of tissues. "Joshie, Joshie, it's going to be okay."

I didn't care how many people looked on, how many tabloids this might end up in. I leaned against Marlene and grieved, the pain as sharp as if my mother had died yesterday.

• • •

I walked past my bike in the parking lot and headed to the pond. I doubted that many of the Bloomies regulars knew about the woods directly behind the store, but I took advantage of the solitude. Fallen leaves covered the ground, crunching underneath my sneakers. (God, how I'd missed New England autumns while I was on the road.) I found a huge pile of leaves under an aging maple and settled in.

Peter, Beth, and the rest of the staff expected a decision; it only made sense. But I felt empty, with nothing left to give our campaign. I rummaged through my bag and took out my ethology textbook. The light began to fade, but I felt comforted by the simplicity of the animal world.

After half an hour I came to one of my favorite passages about the macaques in Japan. Back in 1952, scientists had experimented, leaving sweet potatoes on the island beach where the monkeys lived. One day, a young female macaque took her sweet potato into the water to wash it off. Before that, the monkeys had never ventured into the water, ever. The young macaque's playmate then washed his potato, as did the female's mother. Soon a new tradition evolved. It was as if monkeys had always taken to the sea; all the macaques now washed their sweet potatoes before eating them.[99] The young ones were flexible and open enough to risk trying something new, resulting in a ritual that benefited the entire macaque community forever.

What if the youth of this country—at this moment in time—banded together to hit the voting booths? Years from now, would *all* kids vote, believing that kids had *always* voted? Like that original monkey in Japan in 1952, could a handful of eighteen-year-olds voting tomorrow start a trend that would change history?

I put my notebook away and looked at the pond. The sky screamed red and orange before me. The natural world had

---

[99]Except for the older monkey who resisted the change. Figures.

always nurtured me and now was no exception. The sunset and my animal behavior book made me realize what had taken place in Bloomingdale's a few hours earlier. My mother *had* spoken to me; I just didn't understand what she was trying to say.

I knew what we had to do tomorrow.

And Peter wasn't going to be happy.

ELECTION COUNTDOWN
NOVEMBER 2:
THE BIG DAY

"Nothing?" Peter asked. "That's what you want to do—nothing?"

"It's perfect," I said. "We leave it up to the voters to decide."

Beth dumped her coffee into the sink. "This is stupid, Josh. Let's hold a press conference announcing that we're dropping out of the race and donating the $190 million to a healthcare collaborative. Or setting up scholarships for the needy—"

"I think we *should* hold a press conference," I agreed. "Saying that we trust the people to know the difference between the superficial and the real."

"Look, it sounds like your mom's changed frequencies," Peter said. "But that doesn't mean you have to take her silence literally."

"All along, we've stated that people are smarter than politicians give them credit for, that the wealthy control the media and the media control the polls. What if the polls are wrong? What if people are still behind us 100 percent and could care less about these ridiculous charges?"

"We can't take that risk," Peter said. "You should withdraw or use the money to save the campaign."

"It's my name on the ticket—"

"And mine," Beth added.

"Exactly. That's why I want you with me on this."

She shook her head with so much world-weariness, her long hair swayed behind the chair. "Talk about going out with a whimper instead of a bang. A month ago, I almost thought we had a chance of winning this thing. But now . . ."

It was Election Day, pre-dawn. The dark autumn sky seemed to amplify Beth's sense of impending doom.

She let out a long sigh. "We've been together the whole way on this one. Might as well finish together too."

We left for headquarters where Tim and Lisa joined us in the office.

"Polls open in half an hour," Lisa said. "What did we decide?"

Peter rapped his palms on the table in a drumroll. "Nothing."

"I can't believe you're wonking out," Tim said. "You should decide *something*."

"This doesn't make sense," Lisa said. "We came up with two good plans. You can't do this."

I stood up and stretched to the rafters. "I don't know about you, but I'm going to do something I've never done before in my life." I gave them a huge grin. "I'm going to vote."

Beth shrugged to Tim and Lisa, as if she'd done her best to persuade me and it hadn't worked. The four of them looked ready for catastrophic defeat.

• • •

My neighborhood voted at the local branch of the library. When the town councilman unlocked the doors to the community room at 7 A.M., I was one of many waiting outside in the chilly November air. Peter and Beth would catch up with me later.

I took a sip of my coffee as the woman crossed my name off the town's list of registered voters. It took her a minute to place the name.

"Well, I'm not going to ask who *you're* voting for," she said.

I smiled and headed to the small partitioned area on the left side of the room.

I wanted to scrutinize every candidate and referendum on the ballot but couldn't get past the names at the top of the page: I ran my finger down the list until I got to my own: Josh "Larry" Swensen (Peace).

If I had done nothing else, I had raised important issues. Millions of teens had registered to vote. An eighteen-year-old could actually be president.

I had gotten the word *peace* on the ballot.

I took my pencil and shaded in the small oval next to my name. It didn't matter how much I was going to get torpedoed in this election. I had accomplished a lot.

Back at headquarters, I insisted our staffers continue with our original plans for Election Day: working the phone banks, driving people who had no way to get to the polls, holding up signs at various voting locations. We'd lost several volunteers since the debacle with the offshore holdings, but many were still on board with their original enthusiasm. I knew they were talking among themselves about how we were going to get killed, but I hoped some of their original passion would carry us through the day. Even Simon drove in from Cambridge to help out.

By noontime, the online and television pundits were forecasting east coast results.

"Get ready for this one," the CBS news anchor said. "In our preliminary exit polling, we've got a dead heat. The Republicans with 32 percent of the vote, the Democrats with 30 percent, and the Peace Party's Larry Swensen with 29 percent."

Peter dropped his burrito.

The anchor continued. "Record turnouts in every eastern state thus far, averaging about 78 percent."

The room exploded. Seventy-eight percent! Almost two and a half times more voters than the last presidential election!

I jumped onto the top of the conference table.[100] "I told you people wanted change! I told you they wouldn't be fooled by all the negative type!"

Beth looked like she was headed for anaphylactic shock. She yanked me off the table and pulled me behind the popcorn machine. "You don't think we can win, do you? I am *so* not ready for this."

To be honest, neither was I.

"Don't leave me all day—promise?" she asked.

_____

[100]And proceeded to almost fall.

"Are you nuts? We have to get back out there! We might actually have a shot!"

Tim and Lisa also looked like they needed resuscitation. Luckily Simon remained calm and handed out assignments.

Beth could barely speak. "The west coast just opened. We still have time to make an impact." She got it together enough to set up a speakerphone conference with all the west coast offices.

Me? So much energy surged through my body, I could have run cross-country and visited each Peace Party office personally before the voting booths closed that night.

Peter jingled the keys to the bus in his hand. "Road trip!"

All the available staffers grabbed their coats and raced outside. We piled into the bus, chanting at the top of our lungs.

• • •

By the time evening rolled around, every person on staff was on fire. We headed back to the office to watch the national results come in over the next few hours. Beth, who had rallied thousands of activists for several years, seemed stupefied at the prospect of actually serving as vice president. She and I opted for the quiet of the back room while the others flipped from station to station on the big-screen TV on the stage. I could hear them screaming in the next room; seconds later Lisa appeared.

"Are you ready?"

I told her I wasn't sure.

"We've got 33 percent of the vote."

Beth buried her head deeper into her hands.

"Beth! Get it together!" I yelled.

"Give me some time to adjust, okay? This morning I thought we were going to get killed. Now I've got to think about picking out china for the vice president's mansion."

I looked at her, aghast.

"I'm kidding! Just let me process this."

She was right; the magnitude of the news would overwhelm anyone.[101]

When I finally collapsed from sheer exhaustion, the rubber chicken sticking out from the bottom drawer ratcheted down my emotions. This was Janine's old desk.

I took the chicken out and tried to amuse Beth by making it dance across the printer like the Democratic and Republican committees hearing today's results.

She laughed, one step closer to her old self.

I rummaged through the drawers, looking for any of Janine's other little gizmos. But all I found were folders filled with printouts of old newspaper articles. I took out the folders and read through them.

From the *Boston Globe* two years ago: LOCAL TEEN ADMITS HE'S GURU. Excerpts from my Barbara Walters interview. Photos of the Sagamore Bridge and my bike.

---

[101] I dealt with the anxiety in another way, doodling a map of Gilligan's island on the marker board, laying out where each hut was in relation to the others. It kept my mind off the extraordinary fact that we might actually win.

Beth sidled up behind me. "She must've been curious about your life before her. God, I haven't seen these in ages."

I scanned the articles, many of which I'd never seen. One—an interview with Tracy Hawthorne, a.k.a. betagold— was the most unsettling. Although Tony and Beth had never been able to link betagold to the $190-million sellout, she always flashed into my mind when we talked about people wanting to harm me.

"Ugh, put it away. The fact that Janine actually *met* with her makes me sick." Beth stuffed the pages into the folder and dragged me to the stage.

The 9 P.M. newscaster said the race was still too close to call, but that the number of registered voters who'd showed up today was a record 92 percent.

Peter shook my hand. "All our hard work paid off. No matter who wins."

I agreed with him; no matter who won, *everything* was different.

But as I stared at the pie charts and bar graphs on the television screen, something nagged at me. A word, a name, begging me to scratch it like an itchy scab. What was it?

And just as suddenly, I knew.

I raced[102] through the joyous group to find Beth. She was wringing her hands by the TV with Lisa.

"Where's Tim?" I asked.

---

[102]As quickly as someone can race with a healing femur.

Lisa scanned the room. "I just saw him a while ago with Susie."

Our years of mental telepathy clued Beth in to my thoughts. She shouted at Lisa to go find him.

"It's not that uncommon a last name," Beth said. "Maybe he's not related to betagold at all."

"He was in charge of every scrap of information in this campaign!" I said.

"He had A1 clearance!"

"Which he obviously hacked! I told you it wasn't Janine."

Lisa returned breathlessly and said Tim had left. I grabbed the bus keys from Peter, then Beth and I hurried to the door.

To Tim Hawthorne's apartment.

PART FIVE

"Democratic power is never given; it always has to be taken, then aggressively defended, and retaken when it slips from our hands, for the moneyed powers relentlessly press to gain supremacy and assert their private will over the majority. Today, our gift of democracy is endangered not by military might threatening a sudden, explosive coup but by the stealth of corporate lawyers and politicians, seizing a piece of self-government from us here, then another piece from over there, quietly installing an elitist regime issue by issue, law by law, place by place, with many citizens unaware that their people's authority is slipping away."

Jim Hightower

We made it to Tim's apartment in less than fifteen minutes.

Beth pounded on the door; when no one answered, I threw myself against it until it opened.

The living room was a makeshift office with several banks of computers and monitors. Four different televisions lined one wall, each tuned to a different network. I found the remote and hit mute on all the sets.

"Tim!" I yelled. "Come out here!"

He appeared in the kitchen doorway eating a bowl of cereal. "Did you find the logic bomb on the hard drive?"

I shook my head. "I glarked it was you when I realized what your last name was. Totally redlined my bogometer."

"Too bad you didn't grep the situation a little sooner."

"You had A1 clearance," Beth said. "But I suppose you're the one who entered that information into the MIT system."

He tilted the bowl to his mouth to get the last of the milk. When he came up for air, the little white mustache bugged me so much I almost couldn't concentrate on what he was saying.

"Why'd you do it?" I asked.

He shrugged. "I disagreed with almost all of your platform. Except that everyone should vote—*that* I agreed with."

"People disagreed with me every day. That doesn't mean they wanted to sabotage my campaign."

"Yes, but I *could*. It gave me such a buzz to be in all your top meetings then totally screw you an hour later."

"You could have worked for one of the other candidates," I said. "Done something positive for them instead."

"Let's face it, Larry. Negative sells. Negative works."

"Not for me," I said. "That's one thing I've learned the hard way."

I heard footsteps in the room above us.

"But don't take it personally." Tim lowered his voice. "There were other factors too. My aunt is loaded—never too late to get on her good side, you know what I mean?"

I could hear someone walking down the stairs behind me. I didn't have to turn around to know who it was.

"I hope you offered our guests something," betagold said. "Where are your manners, Timothy?"

She wore a blue tailored suit and carried a suitcase. She still favored that hand cream my mother used to wear, a smell that threw me off guard more than her measured voice.

"This was all you," I said. "Right?"

Betagold nodded, a pleasant smile on her face. "Well I *did* have help. But it was fun to be back in business again."

I thought Beth might push betagold down the stairs; I unconsciously stepped between them.

"Back in the business of ruining people's lives," Beth said. "Of meddling in places you don't belong."

Betagold's eyes twinkled. "When I retired, people told me I should take up a hobby. I thought politics might be fun."

"No, you thought torturing me might be fun," I said.

"Well, I have to admit, tracking you down two years ago *did* give me a great sense of accomplishment. It's important to keep busy. After all, how many episodes of *Matlock* can one person watch?"

"You're giving the elderly a bad name," Beth shot back.

I plopped onto the corduroy recliner. Part of me realized the newscasters on the wall of televisions were about to broadcast the fate of the country along with that of Yours Truly, but I couldn't tear myself away from betagold. "It was never Janine, was it?"

"Good gracious, no. She was just so open, it was easy for Timothy to get whatever information we needed from her."

"And the photograph of you two together?"

"I was asking her for directions—she had no idea it was me. Timothy was kind enough to catch our little meeting on film."

"Janine would have cut off her arm for you," Tim said. "I almost had to leave the room when you yelled at her." He took his suitcase from the hall and set it on the stairs.

"I thought linking everything back to Colorado was quite resourceful," betagold said. "My nephew's idea. Wish I could take credit."

"You both make me sick," Beth chided. "The hit and run—was that you too?"

Betagold looked almost sad. "I had nothing to do with that, I assure you. My employers were just a little too impatient. I tried to warn you."

"Who was behind this?" I asked. "The Democrats or Republicans?"

"It was a real bipartisan effort. If both parties worked this closely in Congress, things might actually get accomplished. They only brought me in for my organizational skills."

"And let's not forget your commitment to the cause," I added.

"True enough. But you really threw a wrench into things with that voter turnout."

"No matter what happens tonight," I said, "people took their power back."

"Talk about setting off the bogometer," Tim said. "You sound like one of the suits."

Betagold reached into her pocket and put on a pair of gloves that matched her outfit. "I want you to know I listened to every one of your speeches and thought you both made several good points. You really did a good job distinguishing yourself from the other parties."

"From you, that's quite the endorsement. I almost appreciate it."

"Are you three done with your little Q and A?" Beth asked. "Because I'm calling the police."

Betagold looked at me knowingly and smiled.

"We can't," I told Beth. "There isn't a shred of evidence

linking her to sabotaging our computers or funneling that money to the Caribbean, is there?"

"Of course not, dear," betagold answered. "You should know me better than that. When the police questioned me after the accident, there wasn't a trace to be found." She moved back the curtain and looked outside. "Timothy, our taxi's here. You two are welcome to stay and watch the returns if you'd like."

"Josh!" Beth screamed. "We can't just let them go!"

Tim picked up their suitcases and opened the front door.

Betagold waved her gloved hand. "I do hope to see you again, Larry. It's always such a pleasure."

She closed the door behind her.

Beth wanted to kill me. "We probably lost the election because of her! She spent months trying to destroy all our hard work! How can you be so calm?"

It was a good question.

Why wasn't I spitting my anger across the room too or throwing betagold's suitcase into the street? Deep down, I knew what the answer was. I had spent the last week analyzing how I'd spoken to Janine, comparing it to the many times Peter and I had exchanged venomous words throughout the years. Being in a different relationship with him now made me realize I didn't want to be a part of that kind of negative energy anymore. I thought about the pact I'd made with myself two years ago—to change myself before I changed the world. Betagold may have destroyed my chance at the presidency, but I never wanted to feel the bitter aftertaste of my own bile again. No matter what happened in the election, honoring that personal commitment seemed like victory enough for me.

Beth grabbed the remote from my hand and hit the mute button. "Do you mind if we find out if we're going to be in the White House next year?"

It was a reasonable request.

She squatted on the arm of the recliner as we watched the faces of the news anchors tally the results.

One reported that 99 percent of the precincts were in and it was time to announce the winner. I had the urge to lock myself in the bathroom and not come out till the broadcast was over.

"In an historic three-way race, Larry Swensen came in third," he said.

I took the remote from the table and hit the power switch, shutting off all the TVs.

Beth flew out of the chair. "Are you nuts? Put it back on!"

I shrugged. "Whoever wins, the people decided. We'll deal with it either way."

"Give me that remote!"

I held it over my head as she tried to grab it, a version of our twelve-year-old selves. She eventually gave in and collapsed on the recliner. She turned to face me. "Are you bummed we didn't win?"

"Kind of. Are you?"

She thought about it for several moments before she answered. "These past few days, I began to fantasize about tackling all those issues we raised at the rallies and really *doing* something about them."

"It would've been great to try," I said. "To be a part of the solution."

"Ninety-two percent voter turnout," she said. "I hate to tell you, but we *are* part of the solution."

I thought of the macaques washing their sweet potatoes as if their ancestors always had.

We had altered our own history. It was almost an honor to be able to make my concession speech.

I grabbed the keys and headed to the door.

"Oh my God," Beth said. "They're waiting for us at head-quarters!"

I had a winner to congratulate and staffers to thank. Not to mention the millions of voters who had changed the course of history.

But as much as I wanted to do those things, there was something I wanted to do even more.

Find Janine.

The post-party was a blur of balloons, confetti, and popcorn. Anyone looking in the windows of the old theater would have thought we had won, and we had. Thirty-seven Peace Party candidates across the country had been elected. Fifty-six eighteen-year-olds had won seats as state senators or representatives. Environmental groups charted a 500 percent increase in volunteers, as did the watchdog groups policing campaign finance reform. Legislators were drafting laws limiting spending during elections. When all was said and done, 96 percent of all youth ages eighteen to twenty-four had voted. And because we'd garnered more than 5 percent of the vote, the Peace Party would be eligible for matching federal funds next election, guaranteeing several promising candidates a running start. And who knows, an eighteen-year-old *might* be president some day. The reporters were eager to cover this wave of active democracy that would keep the new Administration in check.

Me? I called Janine in Boulder, only to find her number disconnected. I flew through my laptop to retrieve my "recently deleted" e-mails. Of the ten or so of hers I'd deleted, only one remained in the file.

SINCE YOU HAVEN'T ANSWERED MY OTHER E-MAILS, THIS ONE IS MY LAST. IF I HAD ONE WISH IN THIS WORLD—EVEN MORE THAN HOPING YOU WIN—IT'S THAT YOU REALIZE I WOULD NEVER DO ANYTHING TO HURT YOU. I LOVE YOU, ALWAYS HAVE, FROM OUR FIRST DATE TO THE HURT IN YOUR EYES AS YOU LASHED OUT AT ME AT THAT MEETING. I'M PULLING A LARRY—SOLD ALL MY STUFF (I'M DOWN TO ONE HUNDRED POSSES-SIONS, COULDN'T QUITE WHITTLE IT DOWN TO SEVENTY-FIVE) AND HITTING THE ROAD WITH BRADY. DON'T WORRY, YOU'LL NEVER HEAR FROM US AGAIN. GOOD LUCK ON ELECTION DAY. LOVE, JANINE. PS: JUST AN IDEA—HAVE YOU CHECKED OUT TIM? I KNOW HIS CRE-DENTIALS ARE STRONG, BUT I'M NOT SURE I TRUST HIM. HE ASKS A LOT OF QUESTIONS. . . .

Beth stood behind the desk, reading the note over my shoulder. "She was good for you."

I snapped my laptop closed. "Yes, she was."

I had something to tell her but didn't know how. I played with the laces of my sneakers and tried to gather my courage.

Thankfully, Beth was more direct. "You can talk to thou-sands of people about issues of national importance, yet you can't look me in the eye and tell me something from your heart."

I was a loser on so many levels, I couldn't begin to keep track.

She dragged her chair next to mine. "You're leaving again, aren't you?"

I nodded and told her I was off to find Janine. I pulled Beth's chair even closer. "The part of you that's my best friend—what does *she* think?"

She tilted her head and looked at me tenderly. "The part of me that's your best friend? That's *all* of me, Josh. Go. I'll be here when you get back."

"Are you sure?"

"I've been around the two of you for almost a year," she said. "I never forced the issue with us because I saw how much she loved you." For once, she couldn't look me in the eye. "More than I did, I'm sorry to say."

As much as I didn't enjoy hearing those words of rejection, there was relief in hearing them too.

Beth punched me in the arm, but not as hard as usual. "I've got to get back to school anyway. If I don't start matriculating, they're going to kick me out."

We held each other for a long time before I headed home.

• • •

There was one person who was going to be almost as hard to say goodbye to as Beth. At dinnertime, I summoned up the courage to tell Peter my plans.

He took it well. "You go find Janine. She's a keeper, that girl."

"For someone who glues Barbie shoes to her sunglasses, she's as solid as you can get."

"Anything you want to do before you go? Bloomingdale's?"

I shook my head. "I barely heard Mom this time around. I don't think she's there anymore."

"She's inside you, always has been. You don't need Chanel to tell you that."

"I thought of her every day on the trail," I added. "She would've had the best ideas."

"They're your ideas now, it's up to you how you use them." He picked up our two plates and brought them to the sink.

It *is* up to me, I thought. *When you ain't got nothing, you got nothing to lose.* But I had something now, several things in fact. A stepfather I loved. A best friend I'd have forever. A girlfriend out there somewhere who deserved an apology.

And a backpack filled with everything I owned waiting by the door.

"Before you go," Peter said. "There's one thing I have to tell you."

"What?"

He looked at me with a crooked smile. "I transferred the offshore money to our account."

"What? You forged my name?"

"Don't worry, the money's already gone. Sent it all to groups supporting election reform. One hundred ninety million dollars from corporate investors going to organizations that fight corporate greed. You've got to love it."

Although I hadn't wanted any part of that dirty money, there was satisfaction in putting cash into the hands of enthusiastic activists working their asses off trying to change the world. Kids like me.

"Stop in and say hi when you're in town, okay?"

I picked up my bag and gave Peter a hug. As much as I'd

miss him, miss Beth, I couldn't wait to get on the road. I thanked Peter for his offer of a lift but headed to the bus station alone.

• • •

At the terminal, I spotted a LARRY/BETH bumper sticker on a vending machine. In the three days since the election, we'd done dozens of interviews; the issues we'd raised were now being talked about by every politician as urgent and necessary. I thought about my late afternoon at the Sagamore eleven months ago, when our entire campaign was nothing more than a note scribbled on a napkin. I thought about how different things would have been if I'd taken that napkin and thrown it away instead of acting on it.

But it wasn't just our successes I thought about; it was the sense of community, the *fun*. Maybe slowly, I was learning to connect to more than just one or two people at a time. Maybe now my journey across the country would be less isolating, more open.

In Springfield, an old man wrapped in several scarves took the seat across the aisle from me. We both nodded our hellos. He reached into one of his bags and pulled out a cribbage board wrapped in a checkered tablecloth.

"You play?" he asked.

I shook my head. "Never have."

He unwrapped the board and placed it between us. "Are you up for learning something new?"

The magic words. I put down my book and smiled. "Absolutely."

Epilogue

Josh looked over the manuscript.

"Wow," he said. "When you see it in black and white, it seems like a big deal."

"Running for president *is* a big deal," I answered.

"It's not like I won."

"What are you talking about? You moved the process miles ahead. Voters realize the enormous power they have."

He picked at the cuff of his shirt. "I was kind of wondering—"

"Of course I voted for you."

His face registered surprise.

"What? You think only young people want change?"

He shook his head. "That's what was so cool. We found out everybody wants it."

We were in my driveway leaning against my car and eating pistachios. Both of us had pink fingers.

He wiped the debris off his shirt and put on his bike helmet.

"Where are you going? My editor's coming at four. You said you'd finally meet her."

"Thank her for me, would you?"

"Are you kidding? You can't leave."

He told me he had a plane to catch.

"Josh, come on. She's going to think I made you up!" I could feel my annoyance rise. I'd look like an idiot if he wasn't here for the meeting. But when I glanced over at him, his smile was so disarming I couldn't give him grief.

"Do you mind dedicating the book to Janine?" he asked.

"Of course not. I'm still hoping they let me put your name on it this time. Or at least a photo."

He shrugged. "It doesn't matter to me either way."

When I asked him to e-mail me his sources, he said he would.

"Speaking of Janine, any leads?"

He shook his head. "I'm heading out west tonight, but I don't have a thing to go on. You'd think someone would remember a girl traveling with a collie. She's better at disappearing than I am."

I told him to send me a postcard and he agreed. He climbed on his bike and secured his pack.

"Am I going to see you again?" I asked.

That great canary-eating smile. "I don't know. Are you?"

I hugged him before he jumped on his bike. When he got to the intersection, he made a left, but not before shooting me a peace sign over his head.

I raised my arm in the air and gave him one in return.

Karl, my fifteen-year-old neighbor, walked by on his way to work. He nodded at my still-raised arm in the air. "You're so sixties sometimes," he said.

"I know. It's a real drawback."

I offered him some pistachios and he took them.

"Was that that Larry guy?"

I told him it was.

"Doesn't he ever sleep? I mean, what fun is it being a teenager if you're worrying about changing the world all the time? The guy needs a life."

I turned to face him. "You know what happens when you try to change the world?"

He shook his head, popped a pistachio into his mouth.

"You usually do," I said.

He jammed his hands into the pockets of his jeans and told me he'd see me around. I spent the rest of the afternoon trying to explain to my editor why she'd come up from New York and Josh wasn't here.

That night I sat on my back steps gazing into the night. Planes flew overhead to and from Logan, one of them carrying Josh to an unnamed city to resume his quest. I watched the planes every few minutes until I just *knew* which one held him. I had no idea what his seat assignment was or where he was headed, but I could feel in my bones he was on that plane.

Later, the television news would be filled with talk of terrorism and corporate looting, but right that minute I felt reassured that thousands of feet above me there was at least one person focused on love and peace. I blanketed that thought around me like wool and took a sip of tea. Tomorrow I would call that citizen group and volunteer my time. Hell, I'd volunteer Karl's time too. But for now, I let my eyes follow this plane across the rooftops and the trees. I leaned back and watched it move through time and space to an expanse of possibilities that seemed hopeful, infinite.

GO FISH

JANET TASHJIAN

What did you want to be when you grew up?
Students ask me this all the time and I wish I had a better answer. When I was young, I was too busy playing, reading, and studying to think about career goals. I envy people who knew what they wanted to be by age ten. I was not one of them.

When did you realize you wanted to be a writer?
My husband and I traveled around the world together, and when we got back to the States, we had to fill in several forms. One asked for 'occupation' and I put down 'writer' even though I'd never done anything more than dabble. But deep down, I always felt being a writer would be the greatest job in the world. It took me several years after that to make that dream a reality.

What's your first childhood memory?
I remember cooking candies in a little pan on a toy stove I got for Christmas. I was maybe three. I'm not

sure if I remember it or if I just saw the photograph so often that I think I do.

What's your most embarrassing childhood memory?
I was singing and dancing in a school assembly with my first-grade class when my shoe fell off. I kept going without the shoe, hopping around the stage—the show must go on.

What was your worst subject in school?
I always did well in school, but for some reason I forgot all my math skills and now can barely multiply. I'd love to know where all my math skills went.

What was your first job?
I've had dozens of jobs since I was sixteen—working on assembly lines, tutoring, babysitting, washing dishes, waiting tables, delivering dental molds and telephone books, selling copy machines, working in a fabric store, painting houses—I could fill a whole page with how many jobs I've had.

How did you celebrate publishing your first book?
By inviting my tenth-grade English teacher to my first book signing. The photo of the two of us from that day sits on my writing desk.

Where do you write your books?
Usually in my office in the house. But because I often write in longhand, I end up writing everywhere—on the beach, in a coffee shop, wherever I am.

SQUARE FISH

Where do you find inspiration for your writing?
Everywhere—there's nothing more interesting or wacky than real life. A word in a book, a bit of conversation in an elevator, something I find in the street. I find dozens of ideas a day. Real life is amazing.

Which of your characters is most like you?
They all have pieces of me. I love words like Marty Frye; I can be a bit obsessive like Monica in *Multiple Choice;* I have the same ambition and persistence as Trudy in *Tru Confessions;* the same striving for the funny as Becky in *Fault Line.* Larry is also very much like me—getting carried away with new ideas while trying to stay focused. We're both big believers in average people trying to change the world.

When you finish a book, who reads it first?
Usually my editor, Christy. Sometimes my husband, Doug. Her feedback is much more helpful; he always thinks what I write is great.

How do you usually feel once you've completed a manuscript? Are you ever sad when a book you are writing is over?
Relieved! I don't really miss my characters; they're always with me.

Are you a morning person or a night owl?
I like waking up early and getting right to work. I'm too fried by the end of the day to get anything substantial done.

SQUARE FISH

What's your idea of the best meal ever?
Something healthy and fresh with lots of friends sitting around talking. Definitely a chocolate dessert.

Which do you like better: cats or dogs?
I love dogs and always have one. I'm allergic to cats so I stay away from them. They don't seem as much fun as dogs anyway.

What do you value most in your friends?
A sense of humor and dependability. All my friends are pretty funny.

Where do you go for peace and quiet?
Like Larry, I head for the woods. I'm there all the time. I love the beach, too.

What makes you laugh out loud?
My son. He's by far the funniest person I know.

What's your favorite song?
Anything by Todd Rundgren, Joni Mitchell, Richard Thompson, or Elvis Costello. Geniuses, all of them. I also love U2's "Bad." I always have a list of songs in mind for every book I write. I wish each book could come with a CD. Music is a very important part of the writing process for me.

Who is your favorite fictional character?
As if I could choose just one!

What are you most afraid of?
I worry about all the normal mom things like war, drunk drivers, and strange illnesses with no cures. I'm also afraid our culture is veering away from basic things like nature. I worry about the implications down the road.

What time of the year do you like best?
The summer, absolutely. I hate the cold.

What is your favorite TV show?
I mostly watch British television. Their comedies are outrageous and their dramas are riveting. I also like anything with Ricky Gervais.

If you were stranded on a desert island, who would you want for company?
My family!

If you could travel in time, where would you go?
To the future, to see how badly we've messed things up.

What's the best advice you have ever received about writing?
To do it as a daily practice, like running or meditation.

How do you react when you receive criticism?
My sales background and MFA workshops left me with a very tough skin. If the feedback makes the book better, bring it on.

What do you want readers to remember about your books?
I want them to remember the characters as if they were old friends.

What would you do if you ever stopped writing?
Try to live my life without finding stories everywhere. For a job, I'd be doing some kind of design—anything from renovating houses to creating fabric.

What do you like best about yourself?
I am not afraid of work.

What is your worst habit?
I hate to exercise.

What do you consider to be your greatest accomplishment?
How great my son is.

What do you wish you could do better?
Write a perfect first draft.

What would your readers be most surprised to learn about you?
I litter McDonald's trash out my car window while I drive—KIDDING!

What is your favorite noise or sound?
My son laughing really hard.

What is your idea of fun?
Walking through New York City at night.

Is there anything you'd like to confess?
I love dark chocolate.

What would your friends say if we asked them about you?
She acts like a fifteen-year-old boy.

What's on your list of things to do right now?
Update my Web site.

What are some things you think about when you're bored?
Story ideas.

How do you spend a rainy day?
Watching comedy DVDs with my son.

Can you share a little-known fact about yourself?
I love to make collages.

*K*eep reading for an excerpt from

Janet Tashjian's **Larry and the Meaning of Life**,

available now in hardcover from Henry Holt.

EXCERPT

There is nothing good on television at three o'clock in the morning. I've spent months doing research; I know. Like a media-fueled zombie, I clicked from channel 02 to 378 then back again, night after night. The programming was dreck, but the images and sounds comforted me. I'd been home for a few months after traveling the country by bus to try and find my girlfriend, Janine.[1] After eight months on the road, I realized she was history. When I returned home, my stepfather, Peter, gladly removed his treadmill from my old bedroom. My best friend, Beth, was less than an hour away at school—I should've been happy. But this was the most miserable period in my life.

Peter tried not to let me see his growing concern. He slapped me on the back and told me I just needed time to settle in. He threw the stack of woe-is-me letters I'd written from the road into the fireplace, setting off a handful of sparks.

"All kids go through this," he said. "Being rudderless at your age is the most normal thing in the world."

---

[1]A quirky girl I'd met in Boulder, Colorado. She never gave me a reason to doubt her, yet I blamed her for the information leak in my presidential campaign. I should've realized betagold—a meddling, upscale senior citizen who outed my Internet identity and stalked me for years—was behind it. One of the biggest mistakes I ever made was believing Janine had betrayed me.

"That's the first time anyone's ever used the *n*-word to describe me."

"See? There's hope for you yet."

I turned toward the fire, avoiding eye contact during yet another humiliating personal conversation. "I hate to sound like a walking cliché, but I don't know why I'm here. I don't know what I'm supposed to be doing with my life."

"Have you tried talking to your mother?"

I told him last time I tried she wasn't there.[2]

"Nonsense. Probably just a bad day. But maybe this will help. Beth's father called—there's a part-time job at the hardware store if you want it."

I'd already bungled my September start date at Princeton and was scheduled to begin classes in January instead. I knew I needed to work between now and then, but I'd replaced the requisite job search with *South Park* reruns. Rerun—I was only eighteen, yet my whole life already seemed like one.

"The hardware store sounds great. I'll call him tomorrow." As much as I'd always enjoyed filling the bins with bolts and mixing paint colors, the thought of getting up, showering, and being at the store by 7 A.M. sent me burrowing deeper into the cushions of the couch.

"Once you get to school, you'll be fine. You're always happiest when you've got a project to keep you busy."

---

[2]My mother died several years ago, but I cooked up a great way for us to talk. I hang around her favorite makeup counter at Bloomingdale's, ask her questions, then wait for people to walk by with the answers. Up until last year, my system worked perfectly. I tried to tell myself the communication technology was just being updated, not that she'd deserted me forever.

"I tried to change the world and failed," I said. "Several times. Just making it through the day is about all I can handle right now."

"I think it's time to talk to a professional."

"A truckload of Prozac couldn't help me deal with how messed up the world is."

"Is that what's bothering you?" Peter asked. "The state of the world?"

"There's conflict on every continent, the poverty rate is increasing, the environment's a wreck, and I'm not supposed to be affected?"

"Maybe you should get involved in solutions instead of sitting on the couch complaining." The touch of anger in his voice reminded me of the old Peter, the workaholic ad exec who'd married my mom.

"I did that, remember? Got my head handed to me on a platter. Spent months writing sermons, spearheading a grassroots campaign for change—nothing."

"You've been through a lot," Peter said. "You're just exhausted."

"I feel like I'm sleepwalking and I'll never wake up."

"I've got to admit I'm worried," he said. "I've never seen you like this." Peter sat with me awhile before going to bed.

It wasn't that long ago my life felt full of purpose.[3] Maybe Peter was right and this was just a blip on the radar screen, a phase that would end once I entered college. But when I really stopped to analyze it, losing the election or the state of the world wasn't the problem— I was. Being so directionless was new territory for me. I'd always prided myself on knowing what I wanted to do: fight consumerism, run for president, change the world. I'd filled notebooks and blogs

---

[3] The purpose might have been twisted, like breaking into the principal's office and downloading the theme from *Jaws* onto his MP3 player for the school awards assembly, but at least there was a purpose.

with ideas and projects since I could remember. Now? I'd tried to write a few sermons since I'd been home but came up dry. Watching an episode of *Family Guy* seemed much easier to manage. And since I stopped hearing my mother's voice at Bloomingdale's, I felt more lost than ever. Talking with her—alive as well as dead—had been a beacon for me, a way of continuing to improve myself and grow. My biological father had died before I was born; for some reason lately, that early loss throbbed like a new wound. If he were alive, would things be different? Peter—at least this recent, caring version—was helpful and kind, but even he couldn't jumpstart my malaise.

When I started the www.thegospelaccordingtolarry.com Web site, some people had called me a guru, but I was the first person to say the term never applied to me. Those long months on the road made me realize I didn't have any answers. And as much as I looked forward to college, it seemed naive to think some professor would take me under his or her wing as a spiritual protégé.

I picked up the remote and clicked—infomercials, Nick at Nite, *The Terminator.* I sank deeper into the couch, hating myself for choosing the wonderful world of distractions over the difficult job of fixing my life.

. . .

"I can't believe you bagged my father," Beth said. "You *love* the hardware store."

"I know—I can't get out of my own way."

"Getting out of your way implies movement. You haven't left the couch in months!"

While studying at Brown this semester, Beth had let a local hairdresser chop and highlight her hair, which was now as short as I'd ever seen it. Surprisingly, the severe style actually softened her expression, tempering the razor-sharp ambition that was usually the first thing you noticed about her. "I can't keep taking the train up from Providence to talk you off the ledge."

"Especially when the ledge is a *Twilight Zone* marathon," I said.

Beth grabbed the remote from my hand and shut off the TV. "Come on, let's go to the woods. Sitting in your hole for a few hours always makes you happy."[4]

I answered her by getting up and turning on the TV by hand.

She shut it off and blocked my path. "This is all because of Janine, isn't it?"

"No."

"Are you sure?"

"Positive."

"Why don't you start a new blog and write a few sermons? You'll feel better."

I told her I'd tried but the words wouldn't come.

"One word in front of the other, like laying bricks," she suggested.

"It's a bigger problem than just writing sermons. It's life in general."

Beth rolled her eyes with exaggeration. "An existential crisis, how unique. You've eighteen, a little too young to give up on life, especially without having lived most of it. You know how much stimulation you need—you're just bored."

I ran through the many projects I'd accomplished since I'd been home: a collage of found objects from the Radio Shack Dumpster entitled *Technical Difficulties*; helping a neighborhood family run a yard sale to benefit Guatemalan refugees; hacking into the town

---

[4]Years ago, it took me a month of afternoons and Saturdays to dig the ten-by-twelve-foot space. It was the setting for many a vision quest and night of solitude—not to mention the place where Beth and I finally hooked up last year.

library's computer system to order several books on astronomy; organizing Peter's books into chronological, alphabetical, categorical order; perfecting a new chocolate dessert; and applying for a patent for my acorn energy processing system.

"And you still have time to sit around and mope?" Beth asked.

"My projects usually motivate me, but now they just feel like fillers to take up time." I lifted the hem of her jeans, exposing her antimaterialism tattoo.

She swatted my hand away and threw me my jacket. "I'm taking out the big guns. We're going to Walden."

I covered myself with the jacket and curled into a fetal position. "I feel like I've let down Thoreau. I can't face him."

She yanked the jacket off me. "Stop being such a baby. He's been dead for a century and a half. I doubt he's worried about your productivity."

I didn't want to admit I'd avoided Walden Pond since I'd been home. Being in a state of mental and emotional disarray at such a sacred spot only added to the torque of my downward spiral.

When Beth forced me to look at her, the expression on her face showed only tenderness and concern. "I'm worried about you."

"You sound like Peter."

"He's worried too."

"You two talked about me?"

"He doesn't know how to help you. Neither do I."

"I'll tell you what you both can do—leave me alone."

She looked at me for a good long time. "On one condition. You at least *try* to help yourself."

"Okay. I'll go to Walden tomorrow. Happy?"

Like the best friend she is, Beth volunteered to come with me.

As much as I would've enjoyed her company, I told her I wanted to experience the pond in solitude. Maybe Henry David could provide some much-needed solace. The thought cheered me up momentarily, until a second one followed right behind it: two of the biggest influences to guide me on life's journey were dead.

. . .

I had to admit it was great to be back at Walden. My body leaned into the earth, relieved to once again be supported by its fertile arms. Watching the orange maple leaves descend to the surface of the pond made me realize there was no other place I'd rather be.

From my favorite spot, I gathered a small pile of acorns and tossed them into the water.[5] I rolled up my jacket, propped it underneath my head, then stretched out on the lush soil. *"Simplify, simplify,"* Henry David Thoreau had written after spending two years, two months, and two days in this sacred palace. Year after year, I kept returning to his words. The advice seemed ridiculously easy, yet in practice proved immensely difficult. Minimizing my number of possessions wasn't a problem—I still logged in at fewer than seventy-five—but reducing the number of distracting thoughts that continually derailed me was next to impossible. I closed my eyes and let the word form a cerebral loop: *simplify, simplify, simplify, simplify, simplify, simplify. . . .*

I was jolted out of my meditation by a middle-aged man with wild gray hair, wearing a dirty Hawaiian shirt and overalls with one side of the denim bib unbuttoned. He stood above me laughing.

---

[5]Why was I the only person besides squirrels to think of using them as an energy source?

"Thinking about Henry David or dreaming about a warm grilled cheese sandwich?"

I told him I'd been thinking about Thoreau.[6]

"All the pilgrims come up here, thinking that if they stare into the green water long enough, their lives will change." He took a knife and small piece of wood from his pocket and began to whittle.

"Is that a rook?"

He held up the small object. "Chess is a great game—a lot like life."

I lay back down on my jacket pillow. "I'd hardly call life a game."

"That's where you're wrong. There are goals, other players, and instructions laid out before you start."

"That's funny, I don't remember reading the inside cover of the box before being born."

"Just 'cuz you don't remember reading the instructions doesn't mean you didn't."

Who *was* this guy?

As if in response, he held out his hand. "Gus Muldarian. Come here every day to walk the pond."

I introduced myself and told him I loved to walk around the pond too.

He unfastened the other button of his overalls. "No, I said what I meant. I walk the pond." He took off his overalls, revealing a patchwork pair of denim cutoffs. His chest and abs seemed as strong as the foundation of a building.

"Be careful, the pond gets deep," I warned.

He took an elastic from the jumble of bands on his wrist and tied back his long hair. "Thoreau himself was the first person to survey the

---

[6] I hadn't felt hungry but could hear my stomach growl after he mentioned the grilled cheese sandwich.

pond—winter of 1846, while it was still iced over—using a compass, chain, and sounding line." He pointed across to the other shore. "The deepest point is over there—a hundred and two feet. I walk as far as I can, but where it's over my head, I tread."

He marched to the shore repeating the sentence like a singsong poem: *Where it's over my head, I tread. Where it's over my head, I tread.* I spent the next hour staring up at the canopy of trees but found myself continually drawn to the water to see if I could spot Gus. He reminded me of some of the wacky travelers I'd met on the road. I couldn't tell if he was Latino, Middle Eastern, Native American, or just plain tan from the remnants of summer. I'd been coming to the pond for years but had never seen him before. My overactive curiosity got the better of me as I stared at his overalls and shirt strewn on the ground. You can tell a lot about a person by what he does—or doesn't—have in his pockets. I made sure he was on the other side of the pond before rifling through his stuff.[7] I unfolded a stained piece of notebook paper and stared at the words scribbled across the page in pencil. Memories flooded in of being stalked several years ago by betagold. I put the paper back in his shirt, grabbed my jacket, and sprinted up the hill. The words haunted me as I ran toward the road. *Josh Swensen.*

---

[7] It's a bad habit, I know.

ALSO AVAILABLE
FROM SQUARE FISH BOOKS